DATE DUE

What Happened to Mr. Forster?

The time: 1958. The place: Kansas City, Missouri.

Fed up with being called "Billy Lou" and feeling like an outsider at school, Louis Lamb determines to make his sixth-grade year different.

The year *is* different, in ways Louis couldn't have anticipated. A new teacher, Jack Forster, takes an interest in Louis, coaches him in softball, and helps him discover his one real talent: writing.

However, parents in the community are suspicious of the bachelor teacher, especially when it emerges that Mr. Forster lives with a male roommate. At the height of Louis's success at school, Mr. Forster suddenly disappears. Louis is desolate; he can't understand what happened to Mr. Forster—or why.

Laced with humor, this is the perceptive story of a young boy's first encounter with the complexities of the adult world.

What Happened to Mr. Forster?

Gary W. Bargar

What Happened to Mr. Forster?

CLARION BOOKS

TICKNOR & FIELDS : A HOUGHTON MIFFLIN COMPANY

NEW YORK

Clarion Books
Ticknor & Fields, a Houghton Mifflin Company

Library of Congress Cataloging in Publication Data

Bargar, Gary W.   What happened to Mr. Forster?
Summary: A sixth grader living in Kansas City in the 1950's
questions the actions of those around him when
one of his favorite teachers is accused of being a homosexual.
[1. Homosexuality—Fiction] I. Title.
PZ7.B25037Wh [Fic] 80-28259 ISBN 0-395-31021-0

For
Florence Gail Norvell,
the first real author I ever knew,
with love

1

September, 1958. The month when Mr. Forster came to teach at Louisa May Alcott School was also the month when I decided I was pretty sick and tired of being called Billy Lou. Everybody called me that. Everybody had *always* called me that. Starting with Aunt Zona.

The first thing I heard every morning was Aunt Zona singing my name. In the half hour before breakfast Aunt Zona never talked if she could sing.

It would start in the kitchen. "Billy Lou. Oh, Billy Boy." Like the opening chord on a piano.

Then Aunt Zona's high-pitched voice, sweet but none too steady, would travel through the dining room, into the hall, around a corner, and toward the back bedroom. "Oh, it's time to get *up*, Billy Boy, Billy Boy. Oh, it's time to get *up*, charming Billy."

By this time I was always wide awake, but there was no use in saying so. Aunt Zona would keep on singing until she reached my room and finished the chorus. If she forgot the words she had made up for the day, she would hum along. But the wind-up was always the same. Aunt Zona would yank the covers off the bed and tickle me in the ribs until I jumped down.

This had been okay when I was seven or eight. But it was no way for an eleven-year-old kid to begin sixth grade, the last grade in grade school. I had been telling her that for weeks.

"Oh, don't tell me you're too big for Aunt Zona to sing to you already! Not my little Billy Lou!"

"No, not your little Billy Lou," I would tell her. "Your big Louis. Call me Louis, Aunt Zona. And talk, don't sing."

After she got through singing, Aunt Zona would lay out my clothes for the day. Most of the time, she wouldn't ask me what I wanted to wear. Then, while I washed and dressed, Aunt Zona would put breakfast on the table.

I had already decided the first day of sixth grade would be different. So the night before, after Aunt Zona was asleep in her room upstairs, I had quietly opened my drawers and taken out the clothes I wanted to wear. When I woke up that morning, there they were, hanging over the bench at the foot of my bed.

I could hear Aunt Zona bustling around in the kitchen. Any minute now, the morning song would start up. I slipped off my pajamas. By the time Aunt Zona began to sing, I had my green flannel shirt buttoned and was pulling on my corduroys.

It had to be different this year, I thought again while I was in the bathroom. I looked down at my favorite floor tile, the one midway between the stool and the

2

sink. If you looked hard enough at it, the black marks on the white tile seemed to spell "Zona." Aunt Zona couldn't see it, even though I'd showed her lots of times where the marks were.

I would be in Mrs. Griggs's class, in Room 3, at the end of the north corridor. I would study world history from the thick blue social studies book all the sixth graders carried around. There would be no bigger boys to collect on the playground after school and shout stuff at me, like "sissy" and "crybaby." I was almost grown-up. There would be no more Billy Lou.

I was even going to walk differently. I would carry my books in one arm at my side, not clutched to my chest like a girl. I might even learn to play softball this year.

I was in the kitchen gulping down Cheerios before Aunt Zona had even finished the first verse of "Billy Boy."

The song died in a sputter of her lips. "Slow down, Billy Lou, you'll get an ulcer." Aunt Zona scratched one of the freckles on her arm in a dissatisfied way, as if she couldn't think of anything better to do. Then she folded her arms and just watched me eat.

I swallowed Cheerios without even chewing. My new notebook and pen were on the table. I grabbed them and headed for the front door.

"Study hard!" Aunt Zona shouted. "Remember, what the hand findeth to do, do it with thy might."

She said a lot more, but one thing I've always been able to do is make a quick getaway.

School was nine blocks away. I ran the first three. But the closer I got, the slower I walked. Would it really be so different this year? Just because I was in sixth grade?

It was almost eight-thirty. I would be right on time.

I walked around to the side of the building, to the door for Room 3. Everyone was there already.

Veronica Allison was talking to a boy I'd never seen before. I didn't expect her to say hello, and she didn't. "Hiya, handsome," Veronica was saying to the boy. She puffed out her hair. "You'd be surprised." Veronica liked to imitate Marilyn Monroe, even though she was chubby and dark and didn't look anything like Marilyn. Standing this close, I could smell the peanut-butter-and-banana sandwiches in her lunch bag.

The boy turned red. He was short—much shorter than Veronica—but the kind of kid the saleswomen in the Boys' Department at Emery, Bird, Thayer called "husky."

"This year," Veronica announced to the boy, the sixth grade, and the world, "I'm going to get myself a *man*."

The new boy looked as though he was about to make a dash for the street. Not that you could run, with every kid in the school standing in the yard waiting for the doors to open.

Robert Goldsmith came over. He was taller and thinner than last year. He stood right in front of Veronica, blocking her out. "Hi," he said to the new kid. "My name's Robert. Are you in Mrs. Griggs's room?"

4

"Yeah," the new boy said. "I'm Paul Harte. We just moved here from Joplin." He whispered, "Who is that girl?" He looked at me, too, when he said it.

So I went ahead and answered. "She's Veronica Allison." Robert Goldsmith looked at me funny, as if he couldn't decide whether I belonged in the conversation or not.

"God, is she weird!" Paul Harte said.

Aunt Zona didn't like people who took the Lord's name in vain. I got a quick chill. Maybe Paul Harte was a hood. He didn't look greasy, though.

"She's got hormone problems," Robert said. Robert always talked about how he was going to grow up to be a doctor. He used lots of medical words.

"She has a phone in her bathroom," I said. It was the most interesting thing I knew about Veronica Allison. Paul looked impressed. Just then, the bell rang.

We all stood there, waiting for Mrs. Griggs to open the door. Mrs. Griggs was a nice teacher. She didn't keep kids after school very much, and she didn't make you answer every social studies question with a complete sentence. I would probably like her class.

The door didn't open. The window shades stayed down. The whole class groaned. Somebody shouted, "Come on, Griggs, open up."

There were two doors to every classroom, an inside door and an outside one. You were supposed to come in from the outside on the first day of school. But now Robert said, "Somebody go inside and see if the other door's open."

"Why don't we go?" Paul said to Robert and me.

Again Robert looked funny. He wasn't used to doing things with me, of course. Then he said, "Okay. Let's."

We started to walk.

"By the way," Paul said to me, "what's your name?"

"Louis," I said, very loudly and distinctly so Robert could hear. "Louis Lamb."

Robert gave me another of those looks. He might have been trying to think of something medical to say about me.

Inside, the door to Room 3 stood wide open. We looked in.

It was incredible. The whole room had changed since last year. The desks were all arranged in circles. Not rows, circles. No teacher at Alcott School ever put the desks in circles. The teacher's desk was shoved off to one side near the windows. Stacks of paper were piled neatly on it. The blackboards all around the room were nearly bare. But one said:

Room 3. Grade Six. Mr. Forster.

Mr. Forster! A man teacher? There were no man teachers at Alcott. Even the industrial arts teacher was a woman.

Another blackboard read:

Thought for the Day
Knowledge is power.
                    Francis Bacon.

6

The handwriting was neat, but kind of flowery. The *p* had an extra loop on it.

Robert and I just stared at it all. Paul said, "I thought the teacher's name was Griggs."

There was a clapping sound behind us. We turned. It was Miss Cobb, the principal. Miss Cobb had fat hands. They clapped loud. In fact, everything about Miss Cobb was fat, except her legs. She reminded me of a marshmallow on two toothpicks. "All right, boys. You know you're supposed to wait outside until your teacher lets you in." She tilted forward on her thin legs. Miss Cobb had scared me when I was young, but now she was beginning to look a little ridiculous. "You three just take seats while I open the outside door. Your teacher will be back in a minute."

She bustled to the door while the three of us sat down in one of the circles. Paul sat between Robert and me. I was glad he'd be sitting next to me.

The rest of the sixth grade filed in. The class got very quiet when they saw the circles. When everyone was sitting down, Miss Cobb said, "Girls and boys, I have an announcement to make. Over the summer Mrs. Griggs's husband was transferred to Germany, so she won't be with us this year. We're very fortunate to have a brand new teacher for the sixth grade."

While she was talking, a man appeared at the inside door. He had thin blond hair, a bit darker than mine, and he was on the plump side. The man crossed the room to Miss Cobb. "This is Mr. Forster, who has come all the way from Alexandria, Virginia, to teach in

Kansas City. I know you'll show him how high our standards are at Alcott School." Miss Cobb gave us all a warning frown. Then she turned quickly and left.

Mr. Forster had picked up a stack of cream-colored manila paper from his desk and was giving a sheaf to each circle. I wondered how you passed paper around a circle—right or left? Sixth grade was beginning to look complicated.

Mr. Forster stood by his desk. It was hard to concentrate on him when he wasn't actually at the front of the room. There *wasn't* a front in Room 3 anymore.

"As Miss Cobb said, I'm Jack Forster." He didn't have much of a southern accent for someone from Virginia. "You all know something about me now, but I don't yet know anything about you. So on this paper, I want you to do two things. On the front, draw a picture of yourself, just the way you think you look. Then, on the back, write down anything about yourself you'd like to tell me."

Hands went up all over the room. Mr. Forster called on Veronica, who had somehow gotten into the same circle as Paul, Robert, and I. "The girl in the pink blouse."

"Well, Mr. Forster," Veronica said, sounding put-upon. "How are we supposed to know what to write?"

Mr. Forster said, "There are no particular rules for this assignment. Just write whatever you think is interesting about yourself."

More kids asked questions, but I decided just to get to work. I wasn't worried about what to write. I could

8

always tell about my china animal collection, and Aunt Zona, and my *Tom Corbett, Space Cadet* books. It was the drawing that bothered me. If I drew myself just the way I thought I looked, I'd look like a very young goblin. I wasn't good at drawing people, anyway.

My Wearever cartridge pen made blurry lines on the manila paper. It was going to be a pretty messy picture.

Mr. Forster walked around the room, not saying much. I wanted to look over at Paul's drawing to see if it was better than mine, but it was hard to tell what Mr. Forster would do. He didn't exactly look strict. But he didn't exactly look nice, either.

The outside door opened. Ellie Siegel stood there, puffing. Even though it wasn't cold, she was wearing a long, navy blue coat with loose threads hanging from the hem. Her white socks wrinkled over ankles that were even skinnier than Miss Cobb's. Robert Goldsmith called in a high-pitched, fakey voice, "Uh-oh, Ellie. You're la-ate."

Mr. Forster gave him the first dark look of the year. "Come in, please," he said to Ellie, "and take a seat. If you hurry, you can finish your paper with the rest of the class."

Ellie looked bewildered, as she always did. For a few seconds she swayed in the doorway. Then she hurried to a desk in the nearest circle. She threw her coat over the chair. Mr. Forster didn't ask her to hang it up. He handed her a piece of manila paper.

9

"I don't have a pencil," Ellie whispered.

Mr. Forster pulled one out of his pocket.

Ellie peeked at the papers of the kids around her, trying to figure out what to do. Mr. Forster let her go on that way for a minute. Then, when she didn't catch on, he leaned over and murmured something in her ear. Ellie blushed and started drawing.

Several kids giggled. Veronica rolled her eyes in a way that made me feel sorry for Ellie already, and the year had hardly begun. Ellie Siegel was always good for another joke.

Mr. Forster began to call the roll. I kept on drawing until he got to my name. "Billy Lou Lamb."

"It's Louis," I corrected. Somehow the words came out much too loud. Mr. Forster raised his eyebrows. More giggles. I felt my face get hot. I was probably bright red, but I didn't care. The giggles were familiar, but this was the new Louis Lamb talking. I wanted them all to know it.

Mr. Forster went right on with the roll. Paul grinned at me, and I felt lots better.

I turned my paper over and began to write:

> *I have a china unicorn that traps the light in its horn. This unicorn knows the secret of a magic dance.*

Mr. Forster gave us almost a half hour to finish our papers. I was in the middle of my third paragraph when I noticed the giggles again. They were coming from around Veronica's chair. Veronica was holding up an index card so that everyone in the circle could read it.

On one side was printed in red:

When she was sure everyone had seen this, she flashed the other side, which had blue writing:

BILLY LOU LAMB IS GOING STEADY
WITH ELLIE SIEGEL.

I was out of my chair almost before I had finished reading the sentence. My paper fell to the floor. I heard myself shouting, "That's a lie, Veronica Allison, and you know it!"

I started over to Veronica's desk. I had to tear up that card, make her take it all back. Veronica Allison was not going to ruin my sixth-grade year on the first day.

A hand gripped my shoulder from behind. Mr. Forster said, "Just a moment. Why are you out of your seat, Louis?"

One of Veronica's friends, Claudia Hardcastle, gave

a romantic-sounding sigh. "Oh, Mr. Forster, Billy Lou's defending his girlfriend's honor."

Mr. Forster ignored her. "I don't care what the problem is, Louis. You are not to get out of your seat without permission. Is that understood?"

I couldn't speak. My eyes started to water.

"I'm afraid you're starting out the year in the doghouse, Louis," Mr. Forster said. "Please hand me your paper, and move your desk into the far corner by itself. You'll stay there until I think you're ready to join the group again."

It wasn't fair. No teacher had ever asked me to sit in the corner, not even Mrs. DeLawter, the fifth-grade teacher, who looked like a cannibal princess and was known to throw books clear across the room. If anyone should be sitting in the corner, it was Veronica.

With everyone watching, I dragged my desk to the corner. The kids in my circle pushed their chairs closer together, so that you couldn't tell that someone was missing. It was as if I'd never sat there.

I was sniffing loud enough for the whole class to hear. Billy Lou Lamb was crying. Same old Billy Lou.

Maybe nothing was going to change, after all. Or maybe this was going to be the worst year ever.

2

"The only good thing about you, Billy Lou Lamb, is your complexion," Veronica Allison was saying. Claudia Hardcastle giggled. We were standing around the outside door, waiting for Mr. Forster to let us in.

Mr. Forster hardly ever arrived until just before the eight-thirty bell rang. Here it was, Friday of the first week of school, and the earliest the outside door had ever opened was eight-twenty. I had told Aunt Zona this, that it didn't matter if I was late to school. It didn't matter if I didn't come at all, but I didn't tell Aunt Zona that. I didn't tell her that I was sitting in the corner, either. Anyway, Aunt Zona still made me come on time.

"How's your girlfriend, Billy Lou?" Claudia asked me.

"Yeah, Billy Lou," Mickey Blake said. "Did you have a date with Ellie last night? How much did you get off her?" Nobody giggled at that, and I was glad. Mickey Blake was practically a hood.

"God, Blake," Paul Harte said disgustedly.

13

"Speaking of dates," Veronica said to Paul. "I happen to be free Saturday night." She pursed her lips, Monroe-style.

Paul looked at an invisible spot in mid-air.

The door opened. "Come in, everyone," Mr. Forster said.

We all filed in. As soon as I reached my desk, I pulled out my library book and buried my face in it.

Out of the corner of my eye, I watched Veronica take *Bartlett's Familiar Quotations* to the blackboard. It was Veronica's turn to put up the Thought for the Day. Mr. Forster made us copy down the Thought for the Day each morning while he took attendance. It was supposed to improve our handwriting. Every day a different person got to choose the Thought. Veronica wrote:

> Thought for the Day
> *What is a kiss? Why this, as some approve:*
> *The sure, sweet cement, glue, and lime of love.*
> >   Robert Herrick.

As she went back to her desk, she let her poodle skirt swirl against Paul's arm. Paul pressed harder on his ballpoint pen but didn't look up.

The tardy bell rang. Mr. Forster closed the outside door just as Ellie Siegel squeezed by it. Ellie scurried to the coat closet and hung up her navy blue coat.

Mr. Forster took attendance while we all wrote down Veronica's Thought. Just as he finished, Ellie dropped into her chair, which rocked for a moment and almost

14

tipped over. The class looked disappointed when Ellie didn't fall out.

Mr. Forster picked up a stack of manila papers from his desk. I recognized them right away. They were the drawings and paragraphs we had done the first day.

"I've had a good time learning all about you the past few days," Mr. Forster told us. "Later this morning, I'm going to hang your pictures and paragraphs on the bulletin board so that you can have the chance to find out more about each other. Some of your papers were so special that I'd like to share them with the class. For instance, here's Paul's self-portrait."

Mr. Forster held up Paul's picture. The boy in the drawing looked confused, just like any new kid in school. He was scratching his head. It looked as if a few flakes of dandruff were falling out. The boy's face was red, like Paul's when Veronica did her Marilyn routine. Everyone laughed. Paul grinned shyly.

Mr. Forster held up several other pictures, but none of them was as good as Paul's. Veronica's drawing didn't look at all like Veronica. The girl in Veronica's picture had about a 38-inch bust and wore one of those slinky skirts with a slit on the side. Robert Goldsmith's picture showed Robert wearing a white coat and carrying something that looked like a fire hose but was probably supposed to be a stethoscope.

"Here are some paragraphs that are especially well-written, even though they're not quite finished." Mr. Forster was holding up my paper. The back of my neck went clammy. "Louis, would you like to read what you wrote to the class?"

He wanted me to read that stuff about Aunt Zona. And my china animal collection! When I read about that, Veronica and her friends would laugh me right out of school. *Have you heard the latest? Billy Lou Lamb plays with little toy animals.*

I had to shake my head no.

Mr. Forster's smile got stiff at the corners. "Are you sure, Louis? I'm sure the class would enjoy hearing your work."

"No, thank you," I said softly. It sounded really stupid. I wasn't surprised when Veronica and Claudia whispered something to each other after I said it. But it would be worse if they heard about the animals.

"All right, Louis. You don't have to read if you don't want to. But how about moving your chair back into a circle? I think maybe you've been holding up that wall long enough."

Several kids laughed. I got up and moved my chair without speaking. I was careful to move exactly where I'd been before, next to Paul.

After that, the morning went quickly. We did mostly English, which was my best subject. Diagramming. I liked to diagram sentences—to draw sharp lines with my ruler and then rest curling, looping written words on them. It was almost like being an artist. I peeked at Paul's paper. Paul did his diagrams in two colors. The lines were black, but he printed all the words in red. I had to admit that his paper looked nicer than mine, even if he did sometimes put his adjectives under the wrong words.

Then it was recess time. For the first few days of school we had free play. I had taken my library book out every day and sat under a tree at the farthest edge of the playground. That had been lonely, but very peaceful. Today Mr. Forster took a softball and two bats out of the teacher's closet.

"Next week we'll be choosing teams for softball," he said. All the boys except me clapped and cheered. My neck got that clammy feeling again—and my stomach, and my hands. "Today, though, I thought we'd do a little practicing—a warm-up for the season. I'll be in the game, too, acting as coach. Just for this morning, I'm going to divide the whole class into two teams. Let's play Circles 1 and 2 against Circles 3 and 4."

Robert Goldsmith's hand shot up. "You mean, play boys and girls together? In the same game?"

Mr. Forster smiled. "That's right."

Most of the boys moaned. A few held their heads in their hands. Veronica sighed loudly. Without raising her hand, she said, "I just hope some big, strong boy shows me how to hold my bat."

— Mr. Forster said, "Class dismissed. I'll meet you on the playground in five minutes."

On the way to the boys' bathroom, Paul fell into step with me. "This really stinks," he said. "Boys and girls in the same game! Do you realize we'll be playing on the same team with Veronica Allison?"

Robert Goldsmith's voice came from behind us,

17

high-pitched and silly: "Ooooh, I do hope some big, strong boy shows me how to hold my bat!"

Paul laughed. I had to smile, too, although I kept thinking about that terrible moment on the playground when Paul would find out what the rest of the class already knew—that Billy Lou Lamb couldn't hold a bat either. Or throw a ball. Or catch one.

Mickey Blake was walking behind us with Robert. As they caught up with us, Mickey cupped his hand and made a quick snatch at Paul's crotch. "Maybe you can show Veronica how to hold it, Paul."

Paul turned red. "Cut it out, Blake!" he snapped.

Mickey Blake put on an innocent, who-me-what-did-I-do look. Then he and Robert started goosing each other. They darted back and forth ahead of us like two basketball players and ran whooping down the stairs to the restroom.

Paul and I followed them down silently.

At the bathroom door, something suddenly occurred to me. My manila paper! Mr. Forster would be hanging it on the bulletin board after recess. Paul would read about my china animals. So would Veronica. And Robert, and Mickey Blake. I had to find that paper and tear it up before Mr. Forster got to it. "I just remembered something. I mean, I forgot something. I'll see you on the playground."

I ran back up the stairs. If Mr. Forster had only left the classroom door unlocked. Yes! Room 3 was wide open. Mr. Forster hadn't learned yet that Alcott teachers always locked up during recess. Miss Cobb

18

didn't want kids sneaking back into the classroom while the teacher was out. She had a very suspicious mind.

The drawings were still on Mr. Forster's desk. No one was in the room—or even in the hall outside. I quickly shuffled through the papers. Where was mine? It didn't seem to be in the stack.

No, there. Sticking out of Mr. Forster's English book. I could tell my handwriting. I pulled the paper out. Mr. Forster had written something on it in red: "Interesting. I like the way you write." I felt peculiar. How could I tear up a paper with something like that on it? I decided just to fold it up and stick it in my back pocket. That way, I could keep the paper, but Mr. Forster wouldn't be able to hang it up.

Still nobody in the hall. I raced back down to the bathroom and outside. Safe! Mr. Forster would never suspect me of stealing my own paper.

I felt so free that I started to skip toward our class's softball diamond. I caught myself just in time. No one had seen me. I would have to be more careful. Billy Lou Lamb might skip, but not me, Louis. Louis Lamb walked straight ahead like a sixth-grade boy.

The game had already started. Mr. Forster was standing out in the field, next to the shortstop, who happened to be Ellie Siegel. Ellie looked scared out of her wits. I couldn't blame her. I only hoped I didn't show it as much as she did.

I walked into the long painted rectangle on the pavement that served as a dugout. Paul was near the front of the batting order, after Mickey Blake and Robert Goldsmith. Then came four or five other boys. All the girls stood together behind them. I was last. If I was lucky, I could get through the first inning without having to be up.

Mr. Forster smiled a lot. When the girls batted, he tried to encourage them. With the boys, he said much less. Our team was doing well, and at first it looked as if I might get my turn.

Then Claudia Hardcastle popped a fly ball, which someone on the other team caught right away. One out. While nobody was looking, I managed to slip back two places in line, behind Mickey and Robert, who had already batted. Nobody on my team cared whether I batted, so they wouldn't stop me.

Veronica actually got a hit. She knew how to hold her bat after all. The ball went straight to Ellie Siegel. Ellie held her arms out stiffly with the elbows almost meeting. You couldn't tell if she was trying to catch the ball or push it away. She missed, and everyone on her team booed her. Mr. Forster frowned. He stopped the entire game while he showed Ellie how to hold her arms to catch a ball. Ellie looked more scared than ever.

While everyone was watching Ellie, I slipped back another place in line. Now I was behind Paul. Paul gave me a funny look, but he didn't say anything.

Mickey Blake made the second out for our team on his second turn at bat. He smacked one over the fence. By Miss Cobb's rules, this was an automatic out. Miss

Cobb didn't like kids having to leave the playground to chase after softballs. She said a truck could run over us, or something. The only truck I'd ever seen pass by Alcott School was a moving truck.

Anyhow, the whole game stopped again while someone ran outside the playground and into the bushes to find the ball.

That was when Mr. Forster noticed me. He started walking toward the dugout. When the pitcher got the ball back, Mr. Forster called to Robert Goldsmith, who had just stepped up to the plate. "Wait, Robert. I don't think Louis has had his turn yet."

My stomach turned over.

"Louis, let's try it."

There was nothing I could do. Everyone was watching. Paul. Mr. Forster. Oh, well.

I walked quickly to home plate to get it over with. I picked up the bat. Mr. Forster came up behind me and positioned my hands. "Like this, Louis. Choke up on it a little." He moved the bat in a wide swing. "And don't forget to follow through."

Mickey Blake said, "You're wasting your time, Mr. Forster. Billy Lou can't hit nothin'."

"That doesn't matter today, Mickey," Mr. Forster said. "We're just warming up. And we could all use a few pointers, couldn't we?"

Since Mickey had just made an out, he pretty well had to shut up.

Of course, Mickey was right. I did strike out.

That meant our team had to go to the field. I was half

afraid Mr. Forster would follow me, but he stayed put. I managed to beat everyone into right field, my favorite spot. Nobody ever hit a ball into right field. While everybody else found a position, I was able to relax. With this many players, the field was too crowded, but that was okay. I just moved further and further back, away from the action.

The other team was a little better than ours. They got quite a few runs, and no outs, before Ellie Siegel came to bat. Naturally, Mr. Forster helped her again.

Incredibly, Ellie got a hit. On the other hand, when she started running to first, Ellie ran just like Ellie. Her legs kicked out from the knee so that she seemed to be running for her life, but she moved very slowly. Her coat flapped around her knees.

Just as Ellie got to first, the pitcher tossed the ball to Mickey Blake, our first baseman. He stepped in front of Ellie to catch it. I was too far away to tell if he tripped her. But right then Ellie fell onto the concrete.

Mr. Forster ran over to help her. Kids started walking toward first. Ellie had ripped a pretty bad gash in her leg, and she was squealing her head off.

Mr. Forster tried to calm her down, but Ellie only cried louder.

"Veronica, Claudia," Mr. Forster called. Veronica and Claudia came slowly in from center field. "Help Ellie to the nurse's office, please." Veronica and Claudia got on either side of Ellie, looking very sour. Ellie pushed them away and limped off into the school building, sobbing all the way.

That finished the game. Mr. Forster lined us up, and we went back to class. Behind his back, Mickey goosed Robert and Robert goosed Mickey. Both of them tried to goose Paul, but he got away.

As soon as we got to the room, I started worrying. What if Mr. Forster started to hang the manila papers now? What would he say when he found out mine was missing? But Mr. Forster didn't touch the manila papers. Instead, he started us on arithmetic.

I had forgotten all about Ellie, until she limped in with a bandage on her leg while we were doing a set of multiplication problems.

"My mother is coming to pick me up," she said. She was really saying it to the whole class, but she only looked at Mr. Forster. "I might have to have an x-ray."

At that, Robert Goldsmith made a loud, rude noise. Good thing he wasn't Ellie's doctor.

Mr. Forster looked puzzled. "What did the nurse say? Is your leg really that bad, Ellie?"

Ellie said, "My mother thinks I should see a doctor." She limped to her desk and sat down with her coat still on.

Mr. Forster started to say something else, then he seemed to change his mind. We went on with arithmetic. Ellie just sat there. She didn't take out her arithmetic book, or anything.

Just before lunch the inside door opened. Mrs. Siegel stalked into the room. Mrs. Siegel was the kind of mother who comes to school a lot. She was as thin as Ellie, but older and tougher looking. Mrs. Siegel wore the brightest, reddest lipstick in the world, only the shape of it was off—as if she had tried to paint someone else's mouth on top of her own.

Mrs. Siegel glared at Mr. Forster. "This is a fine kind of way for my daughter to be starting a new school year," she said loudly. "I'd like to know what kind of teacher forces a little girl to play baseball with rough boys. Is that your idea of physical education, Mr. Forster?"

Everybody stopped writing. The room was deathly quiet.

Before Mr. Forster could say anything, Mrs. Siegel snapped her fingers at Ellie. "Well, come on, hurry up. I don't have all day to stand here waiting." Ellie rose slowly and limped to the door. "You'll hear from me later," Mrs. Siegel called back at Mr. Forster as they went out.

Mr. Forster didn't speak for a minute or two. The lunch bell rang, and Mr. Forster closed his arithmetic book. "All right, class. I think we're all ready for a break."

3

Love lifted me. Love lifted me.
When no-o-thing else could help,
love lifted me . . .

I t was Sunday morning. I could tell that before I even opened my eyes by Aunt Zona's song. From practically the minute she got out of bed on Sundays, Aunt Zona started rehearsing for church. Not that she sang in the choir or anything. Aunt Zona just liked to be sure she'd be able to sing the hymns good and loud.

Aunt Zona's head popped through the doorway of my room. "Billy Lou, rise and shine. This is the day that the Lord hath made. What would you like for breakfast—french toast or pancakes?" Without waiting for an answer, Aunt Zona breezed through the room and pulled my good suit out of the closet.

"I can do it, Aunt Zona," I grumbled.

"All right, punkin. But make it snappy. Sunday School's in less than an hour."

I could smell french toast frying in the kitchen as I got up. Aunt Zona was doing better—at least she let me choose my own shirt and tie now. Even after I was

25

completely washed and dressed, I couldn't stop yawning. Why was it so much harder to get up on Sunday morning, even though I could sleep a whole hour later than during the week?

I didn't really mind going to Sunday School at the New Jerusalem Baptist Church. I just wished it were held in the afternoon. Reverend Hardcastle always said that a really good Christian goes to church morning and night, every Sunday, and to Wednesday night prayer meeting, too. But Aunt Zona said that the Lord would forgive us for only going on Sunday morning, as long as we prayed three times harder than we did the rest of the week.

Aunt Zona stood over me the whole time I was eating my french toast. She was wearing her best pink dress, and her permanent was fresh and springy.

"You've got powder on your dress," I told her, chewing.

"Don't talk with your mouth full. Where is it?"

"On the collar. See?" I brushed the spot.

"Much obliged." Aunt Zona whisked my plate to the sink and rinsed it. "You got your Bible?"

I had forgotten it. I ran back to my bedroom. My Bible was next to the photograph of my mother on the dresser. A piece of manila paper was sticking out of it. That was where I had hidden the paper I took from Mr. Forster's desk. As quietly as I could, I opened a dresser drawer and slipped the paper under some shirts.

"Billy Lou!" Aunt Zona's voice came from the direction of the front door. "Come on, come on, come on." I raced to join her. "Molasses!" she cried, giving me a light tap on the fanny.

As usual, we walked to church. It was only about six blocks from our house. At the north door, we separated. Aunt Zona went upstairs to her Noble Ruths class. Most of the people in that class were widows, like Aunt Zona. Some of them were pretty old. Reverend Hardcastle's mother was over ninety. Next to her, Aunt Zona looked young.

I went downstairs to the sixth-grade class. The Young Galileans. Reverend Hardcastle's wife taught that class. Mrs. Hardcastle was standing at the classroom door beaming as I came in. Mrs. Hardcastle was the only woman I knew who wore a wig. Today the wig seemed a little tilted. Of course, you could never mention that to her. Sometimes I wondered what kind of hair Mrs. Hardcastle really had under her wig. Maybe she was bald. Mrs. Hardcastle was Claudia Hardcastle's mother, and in my opinion, that would be enough to make anyone's hair fall out.

Most of the class was already there. Some of them were people I saw all during the week: Claudia, Mickey Blake, Veronica Allison.

"Hi, Billy Lou," Claudia said sweetly.

I sat down as far away from Claudia, Veronica, and Mickey as I could get, at the other end of the room, next to Wanda Sue Grier. Wanda Sue was very fat, and I thought she might help keep me out of sight.

"Claudia said something to you, Billy Lou," Mrs.

Hardcastle said in the same sweet tone Claudia had used.

"Hi, Claudia," I mumbled, and looked away.

Mrs. Hardcastle closed the door. "Let us pray." Even though we were praying, and I really was supposed to have my eyes closed, I couldn't help staring at Veronica's outfit. Veronica was dressed all in black. Black turtleneck sweater. Black slacks—and girls never wore slacks to church! Black slippers, too. She looked like a ballet dancer on her way to a funeral.

Mrs. Hardcastle didn't seem to notice. Or, rather, she deliberately kept from noticing. While Kenny Edwards and Brent Kramer passed out this week's Sunday School papers, she kept her eyes fixed on the window. Nothing interesting was happening outside that I could see.

We read the papers quietly for a while. This week's story was about a girl who forgives her sister for stealing her best hair ribbon. Stealing. That made me feel uncomfortable. Hadn't I stolen something lately from Mr. Forster? Well, not exactly. How could it be stealing to take something that was yours to begin with?

"Billy Lou Lamb!" Mrs. Hardcastle was talking to me.

"Yes? What?"

"I said, would you please read this morning's Scripture aloud? Matthew 24:29–30."

Everyone else had found the place. I flipped the pages of my Bible quickly. "Immediately after the tribulation of those days shall the sun be darkened,

28

and the moon shall not give her light, and the stars shall fall from heaven, and the powers of the heavens shall be shaken:

"And then shall appear the sign of the Son of man in heaven; and then shall all the tribes of the earth mourn, and they shall see the Son of man coming in the clouds of heaven with power and great glory."

"That's right." Mrs. Hardcastle started talking about the Scripture. About how Jesus would come again at the end of the world, and how everyone would be judged. "Sometimes I think about that day, and how I'll stand before the Lord myself," Mrs. Hardcastle told us. "And he'll look at me through rays of glory. And he'll say to me, Xenia. Xenia Hardcastle, what have you done that you should inherit a share in the kingdom of heaven?"

I squirmed in my chair. I didn't like today's lesson much. It made me think more about stealing the paper from Mr. Forster's desk. That didn't sound like the kind of thing Jesus would want me to do. I didn't think I wanted him to come back today and ask me about that. I glanced out the window to check on the clouds of heaven. Luckily, they didn't seem to be mounting up any more than usual. But who could tell when the Lord would decide to come again? The Bible said it could be any time. Why not today?

Mrs. Hardcastle talked for quite a while. Toward the end, she began to get more and more excited. Her face got red, and her wig slipped further down. Finally she said, "And now, boys and girls, let's all think of a way we can please Jesus better in the coming week. Just think of one good deed that you can do for the Lord. Think real hard." Mrs. Hardcastle stopped for a minute to let us think. "Now I want each of you to tell the class what one thing you've decided to do for Jesus this week."

For a minute I thought about heading for the door. But where could I go? Anyway, if I ran out of Sunday School, Aunt Zona would be sure to hear about it. I couldn't tell about taking the paper from Mr. Forster, even though putting it back might be a good way to please Jesus. I'd just have to make something up. But then, that would be a lie, and a lie surely wouldn't please the Lord.

But Mrs. Hardcastle wasn't looking my way. She was looking at Veronica. "Well, Veronica, what have you decided to do?"

Veronica smoothed her black slacks. "I really couldn't say, Mrs. Hardcastle. I'm thinking of becoming an atheist."

Mrs. Hardcastle's jaw dropped. "What's that?"

"An atheist," Veronica repeated. "That's somebody who doesn't believe in God."

"I know what the *word* means, Veronica Allison. I just can't believe that I'm standing here in this room, not ten feet below the spot where you were baptized, hearing you say what I just heard you say."

"Well, you see, I've been reading this book at school, all about evolution. And if people came from monkeys and apes, like the book says, then I don't see what God had to do with it. So I don't believe in God anymore."

"At school!" Mrs. Hardcastle opened her mouth wide, as if she were trying to get her breath. "Does your teacher know about this book?"

Veronica shrugged. She seemed to be enjoying herself. "He'll find out about it on Monday when I give my book report."

"Is that right?" Mrs. Hardcastle said. "Well, I don't see how any teacher with any sense at all would let a student make a report on that kind of book."

Claudia said, "Oh, we get extra credit for every book we read, Mama."

"Extra credit!" Mrs. Hardcastle folded her arms tightly together. She sounded as if she had just heard the worst news of all.

Out in the corridor there was a lot of noise. People were leaving their classes and heading upstairs for the church service.

"Veronica, is your mother here with you today?"

"Oh, no, Mrs. Hardcastle. She and my father are out of town on a business trip. I'm staying with my grandmother this weekend."

"I see. Then I guess I'll just have to talk this over with her next week."

Veronica blushed and whispered something to Claudia. Claudia nodded.

There was nothing for Mrs. Hardcastle to do but let us out of class. On the way out, Wanda Sue Grier tapped Veronica on the shoulder. "Why are you wearing those clothes?" Wanda Sue asked.

31

Veronica kind of sniffed at her. "I'm going to be an actress," she said. "Like Tuesday Weld. This is how actresses always dress before they're discovered."

"Really?" Wanda Sue said. "Well, gosh. Good luck."

"Thanks."

I wanted to tell Veronica how crazy I thought she was. But on the other hand, Veronica had just done a good deed for me. Because of her, Mrs. Hardcastle hadn't called on me, and I hadn't had to tell about the stolen paper. So I didn't say anything. Veronica and Claudia sashayed off.

Aunt Zona would be waiting for me at the sanctuary door. I ran up the stairs two at a time.

4

The weather was nice, so we stopped at the Dairy Deelite on the way home from church. Aunt Zona ordered ice-cream cones for both of us—vanilla. "The Lord won't mind us having a lick or two of vanilla," Aunt Zona told me—and the boy in the white suit behind the window of the Dairy Deelite stand. "But no fancy flavors on the Sabbath."

Vanilla was just fine with me. We walked down Prospect Avenue, licking our cones. "How was Sunday School?" Aunt Zona asked.

"It was okay. Veronica Allison told Mrs. Hardcastle that she doesn't believe in God."

"You don't mean it!" Aunt Zona bit an extra big mouthful out of her cone, as if she couldn't stop herself. "Right in the house of the Lord?"

"Mrs. Hardcastle said that she was going to tell Veronica's mother."

"Oh, that won't do any good. That poor Miz Allison never did have a bit of control over those children. You remember that older brother who got in trouble."

Veronica's brother had stolen a car once, but he hadn't had to go to prison. He was only sixteen.

"It's all the martinis those Allisons drink. Some people get money, and they just fall all to pieces." Veronica's parents owned a chain of dry cleaning stores, and they were pretty rich. They had two Buicks. "You have to set an example for the children. Of course, it's not our place to judge. They love those kids, same as I love you." Aunt Zona gave my shoulders a hard squeeze. I could scarcely break loose.

"I just don't know how anyone can say they don't believe in God," Aunt Zona said a few minutes later. "When I think of all the wonderful things the Lord has done for me. I lost both my parents before I was twelve. Lost my husband after twenty-six years of marriage. Your Uncle Emmett. Lost my baby sister, too." That was my mother. "But I never said a prayer that the Lord didn't answer. Never once."

"How do you know he answered?" I asked Aunt Zona. "Did you hear a voice?"

Aunt Zona frowned. She rubbed some ice cream off the corner of her mouth. "The Lord works in mysterious ways. He doesn't always answer you the way you expect. Sometimes he just speaks to you in your heart."

Now my heart was beating faster than usual. I didn't want any voices coming into me through my heart.

"And look at all he's given me! I've got my health. I've got my home. And I've got my sweet Billy Lou." Here Aunt Zona gave me another crushing hug, quick before I could get away. Then she began to sing: *Count your many bles-sings, name them one by one . . .*

By the time she got through two choruses, we were home.

I went straight to my room and didn't come out, except for dinner. First, I reached into the dresser drawer under my shirts where the manila paper was. Still there. I started to take it out. Then I changed my mind. I closed the drawer again, quietly, so that Aunt Zona wouldn't hear.

I spent the afternoon playing with my china animals. With the door closed, of course. I didn't want even Aunt Zona to see me. I spread them all out on the floor under the back window.

The unicorn was my favorite, because he was beautiful. And pure. The afternoon sun glanced off his strong white back. He fought with the lion, and he always won. The tigers were afraid of him. The giraffes ducked their necks when he passed. Even the rhinoceros bowed to him. The rhinoceros had lost his horn a long time ago. He was ashamed to look at the unicorn.

I lined all the animals up. Together they formed a snake that stretched across my bedroom floor. When the shadows in my room were just right, their muscles seemed to ripple. The line began to shift. I closed one eye, and then the other, and the animals started to dance.

I stood in the center of my bedroom while the animals paraded around, the unicorn dipping and curtsying at the head. And the line became a circle, and the circle made a barrier. An unbreakable barrier. I was surrounded by the dancing animals, safe in the midst of them.

Now and then I looked out the window. At the clouds in heaven. My heart beating.

From the dresser, my mother's picture smiled at me. The picture had been taken when my mother was very young, about my age. Her hair was a frizzy platinum blonde. She was wearing a frilly dress and tap shoes. Aunt Zona always said my mother had been a regular little Shirley Temple. I stared at the picture for a while.

It was getting dark when Aunt Zona knocked on the bedroom door. "Billy Lou! Come out, come out, wherever you are. There's chicken sandwiches on the table and chocolate milk to drink. And pretty soon it'll be time for Ed Sullivan."

The chicken sandwiches tasted terrible. And I couldn't concentrate on Ed Sullivan.

"What's wrong, punkin?" Aunt Zona asked me during one of the commercials. "You're not coming down with something, are you?"

"No."

She felt my forehead anyway.

"Excuse me," I said. I went back to my bedroom and took the manila paper out of the drawer again. I walked over to the wastebasket and tore the paper into tiny pieces. No one would ever read it again. But tomorrow morning I would tell Mr. Forster what I had done. At least I would do that. I would tell him the truth.

36

On Monday morning the bulletin board was full of manila papers. As I walked into the room, I glanced at Mr. Forster. He must have found out my paper was missing by now, but he just smiled at me as if nothing were wrong. I started to take a step toward his desk, then I changed my mind. I could wait and talk to him at recess.

Paul put up the Thought for the Day. He wrote:

> Thought for the Day
> *Beneath this stone a lump of clay*
> *Lies Uncle Peter Daniels*
> *Who too early in the month of May*
> *Took off his winter flannels.*
> Epitaph, Medway, Massachusetts.

"That certainly is a weird Thought for the Day," hissed Claudia Hardcastle, as Paul sat down in his chair.

"I like it," Paul said.

"So do I," I told him. "It's a whole lot better than Veronica's Thought, anyway."

Paul looked at Veronica. He crossed his eyes at her. Then he turned to me and made crazy wheels on his forehead with his index fingers.

Veronica was still wearing her all-black outfit. If you looked twice, you could tell that she had put on a dab of lipstick and rouge. So had Claudia. I wondered how Claudia had managed to get out the door this morning without Reverend or Mrs. Hardcastle wiping that stuff off.

37

Right after the tardy bell rang, Ellie Siegel appeared at the outside door. She was wearing an enormous bandage on her right leg. As she passed my desk on her way back from hanging up her coat, I could see that the bandage had brown streaks on it.

Mr. Forster didn't even wait for Ellie to sit down. "Who has a book report today?" he asked.

A bunch of kids raised their hands, including Veronica. The first two reports were dull. Ricky Culligan was reading his umpteenth Space Cat story. Georgia Smith gave a report on a ballet book. She showed us seventeen pictures from it. When Georgia was finished, the floor was littered with crumpled pieces of yellow paper she'd been using as book markers. We had to wait another five minutes while Mr. Forster made Georgia pick all the markers up.

Then it was Veronica's turn. Veronica was trying to walk slinky. To me, she just looked like someone with a bad back.

Veronica cleared her throat. "My report is on *Darwin's World.*" She held up a thick book. I couldn't believe Veronica would read something that long. "Charles Darwin proved that people are descended from apes and things. This is called evolution." Veronica slunk over to the blackboard and wrote the word *evolution*. As her talk went on, Veronica kept writing. She wrote *natural selection, survival of the fittingest, H.M.S. Beagle,* and *The Decent of Man.*

At the end of the talk, Veronica said, "And because of this book, I have decided to become an atheist. Because, after all, creation took millions and billions of eons, which is a lot longer than seven days, like in the Bible. And I would rather be descended from apes, anyway, because monkeys are smart. But Adam and Eve were just plain dumb to listen to that serpent, so who wants to be descended from *them?*"

Veronica took her seat.

Mr. Forster made funny noises—as if he had something caught in his throat. Finally he said, "Thank you, Veronica. I'm always pleased when students stretch their minds by reading difficult books." Veronica preened. "And you're certainly entitled to form your own opinions about creation and evolution. Personally, I think you're being a little hard on God." Veronica stopped preening. "It seems to me that if Darwin's theories are true, then evolution is still going on. That means God spent billions of years on his creation, and he isn't tired of it yet. He's still creating. I think that evolution makes God even more interesting and wonderful."

Claudia Hardcastle raised her hand. "Mr. Forster," she asked, "are you a Baptist?"

"No," Mr. Forster said. "I was raised a high-church Anglican."

I wondered what in the world a high-church Anglican was. I tried to picture Mr. Forster back in Alexandria, Virginia, climbing a steep hill every Sunday morning to get to church. I decided to ask him about that later. Maybe there were lots of hills in Alexandria with a church at the top of every one of them. And people lived in the valleys.

Veronica pouted all morning.

At ten-thirty Mr. Forster had us put our books away. "Today we're going to choose softball teams," he announced. I wished I had my library book out and could hide behind it while all this went on. I knew what would happen. I would be the last boy in the room chosen for a team. Then I would go out to the playground and strike out all week.

Mr. Forster let the girls choose their teams first. "At least we don't have to play with *them* anymore," Paul whispered to me. I tried to look glad. Actually, it was more fun to play with the girls. At least most of them didn't care whether you made a home run or not.

Then it was the boys' turn. Mickey Blake and Robert Goldsmith were elected captains. They got to take turns calling out the names of the guys they wanted on their teams.

It happened the way it always did. First there were eighteen boys sitting at their desks. Then guys stood up behind either Mickey or Robert as their names were called. Sixteen boys still sitting. Fourteen boys. Twelve. By the time only six of us were left, our faces got very stiff from looking as if we belonged in another class and couldn't see or hear what was going on in this one. Four boys left. My throat began to hurt. It was important not to swallow until you were out the door. Two boys left—it was almost over. Finally Robert chose Frankie Burns, who had asthma and was absent half the time. That meant Mickey was stuck with me. I didn't wait for him to call my name. I just walked out the door.

I stayed away from everyone on the playground. It didn't matter whether I was in the dugout. Mickey wouldn't check up on me. Besides, I was waiting for Mr. Forster to come out. Now was the time. I had to talk to him about that paper.

Mr. Forster showed up late. He stood in a corner of the playground under the branches of an old elm tree that grew next to the fence. Now and then he checked his wristwatch. He kept tapping his foot.

Gradually, I edged toward the old elm. Mr. Forster was wearing dark brown loafers. The toes were scuffed, and there were frayed leather tufts on the insteps. I looked at the tufts while I talked. "I have to tell you something, Mr. Forster."

His foot stopped tapping. "All right, Louis. What is it?"

"Um." I wiped my palms on my corduroys. "Um. I'm sorry. I mean, I took something off your desk and I'm sorry."

Mr. Forster didn't say anything.

"My paper. The paper I wrote on the first day of school. I took it back. I'm sorry."

Mr. Forster coughed.

"I didn't want anyone to read what was in it, so I took it home and tore it up. I'll write you another one, though, if you want. Two papers. I'll do two papers as a make-up."

41

I looked up at his face. I had to. My neck was getting tired. "I'm really sorry, Mr. Forster." The words were running all together. Tears were coming into my eyes. "It's stealing, I know, and I'm really very, very sorry."

"Louis, it's all right," Mr. Forster interrupted me. "I knew all along that you took the paper. And I understand why. It was my fault, really. I pushed you into it by pressing too hard. Of course, you have the right to keep your work private—if you want to. Always. You don't have to share anything with the class unless you want to."

Luckily, Aunt Zona had packed my pockets with Kleenex this morning. I took one out and blew.

"I tell you what. If you want to do a make-up assignment, write me something completely different. Invent a character of your own. Write *his* life story. It can be just the opposite of your life. Anything goes." Mr. Forster was grinning now.

I sort of grinned back. "Okay," I said. I couldn't get any more words out. I didn't know what I was going to write, but I'd make it good for him.

Up close, Mr. Forster didn't smell like a teacher. He smelled a little like stale cigarette smoke, and a lot like some kind of after-shave I'd never smelled before. It was minty. Not at all like Old Spice, which my Uncle Emmett used to wear.

"I have been waiting in that office for nearly twenty minutes, Mr. Forster." I turned around. Ellie Siegel's mother was standing behind me. Who knows how she'd managed to sneak up so quietly.

42

"Oh, Mrs. Siegel. Good morning." Mr. Forster coughed. "I think perhaps we had our signals crossed. *I* was waiting in the classroom for *you*."

Mrs. Siegel's red, red lips twitched as if she didn't believe a word he was saying. "I'm in a hurry," she said. "I have a beautician's appointment."

"Of course. Just one more minute." Mr. Forster looked back at me. "Louis, I was just wondering. Do you think it might help if I gave you a little extra coaching in softball? We could practice after school, if your aunt doesn't mind. Just to make recess more— enjoyable—for you."

I blinked at him. "Well . . ." I didn't think any amount of extra coaching could help my softball game. But then again, Mr. Forster was trying to be nice. And he'd probably give up after a few lessons, anyway. "I guess that would be all right. I'll ask Aunt Zona at lunch."

"Good." Mr. Forster gave me another of his grins. His eyes crinkled up at the corners when he grinned like that.

"Just any time you're ready for our talk, Mr. Forster," Mrs. Siegel said.

The two of them went into the school.

5

It took me a long time to explain to Aunt Zona why I was staying after school. "You're sure you're not in some kind of trouble?" she kept asking me. After a while she said, "Well, just you be home in time for supper."

And so my softball lessons with Mr. Forster began. We practiced on the playground almost every day from 3:30 to 4:30. It turned out Mr. Forster had been the softball coach at his last school. Virginia Episcopal Preparatory Academy for Young Men. An all-boys school.

Mr. Forster started out by working on my catching. Catching was already my best subject, as far as softball went. On a good day, I could catch about half the balls Mr. Forster threw.

"Don't duck, Louis!" Mr. Forster called out as he tossed them to me.

Once a fast one clipped my ear, and we had to quit for almost ten minutes while I waited for the ringing to stop

"How come you decided to move to Kansas City?" I asked Mr. Forster as we sat under the old elm. Then I wished I hadn't. It sounded nosy.

Mr. Forster was chewing a blade of grass. Without taking it out, he said, "I needed a change of scenery. After all, I lived in Virginia most of my life. It was about time to see some of the rest of the country." Mr. Forster rolled the grass over and over on the tip of his tongue. "Besides that, my best friend got a job with the *Kansas City Star*. He's a reporter."

"Really? Maybe I've seen his name in the paper."

Mr. Forster jumped up. "No more lazing around under the trees, Louis. We've got a lot more work to do."

On the fifth afternoon, we switched to batting practice.

This was harder than catching. The way it worked, Mr. Forster would pitch the ball to me. I'd take a swing at it. I'd miss. Then I'd drop my bat and run after the ball. I'd throw it back to Mr. Forster. He'd wind up and pitch again. I'd miss again.

After a half hour of this, somebody shouted, "Hey, Louis, Mr. Forster." Paul Harte pedaled onto the playground on his bike.

Mr. Forster waved.

Paul pulled up next to me. "What's all this?" Paul asked me.

"We're, um, practicing." My face burned.

"You won't get very far that way," Paul said. "You need a catcher."

45

"You're not volunteering, are you, Paul?" Mr. Forster asked with one of his grins.

"Sure!" Paul parked his bike against the school building. He positioned himself behind me. "Fire away!" he told Mr. Forster.

"Warm up first," shouted Mr. Forster.

I got out of the way while they tossed the ball back and forth. Paul wasn't one of the best players in the class, but he was a whole lot better than I was.

"Okay, batter up!" Mr. Forster called to me. We started up again. I still kept missing, but now Paul was there to catch the ball right away, so things moved faster.

Once I actually tipped the ball. It went about three feet.

"Nice bunt!" Paul cried.

Mr. Forster gave me a big smile.

I didn't tell them I wasn't bunting.

"One more day like today and we'll be in business," Mr. Forster said as we carried the bat and ball into the classroom.

"Yeah, Louis. You're really not so bad," Paul said.

We walked Mr. Forster to his car, a blue Chevrolet with a thick coat of dust on it.

"If you want, I'll practice with you again tomorrow," Paul offered.

"How about it, Louis?" Mr. Forster said. "We could use him."

"Sure." I felt my face turn pink again.

"I won't tell anyone what we're doing," Paul said.

"We'll get you all shaped up and surprise Blake and Goldsmith and those guys."

Mr. Forster honked at us as he drove off.

"Want a ride home?" Paul patted the back fender of his bike.

I climbed on.

Paul must have had strong legs. We went pretty fast, with me holding on to the back of the seat. I did have to push the bike part of the way up Fifty-fifth Street. Still, it didn't take us long to get to my house.

Aunt Zona was sitting on the front porch swing. "Well, hello, stranger," she yelled at me. "Now who's this young man with you?"

So I had to take Paul up and introduce him.

"I'll bet you boys worked up an appetite on that playground," Aunt Zona said. "How about some homemade chocolate brownies with ice cream on top? A la mode! Just like Peck's soda fountain."

Paul said, "I don't know, Mrs. Crenshaw. It's getting pretty close to sup—"

Aunt Zona was already on her way into the house. "A good homemade brownie never hurt a growing boy." The screen door banged behind her.

We sat on the porch steps. After a minute, Paul said, "Your aunt's pretty nice."

I nodded.

"Kind of a crackerbox, but nice."

I nodded again.

"How come you live with her? What happened to your mother and father?" Paul asked.

"My mother died when I was two."

"What about your father?"

I chewed my lower lip.

"Why don't you live with him?" Paul said.

"I don't know. I've never met him."

"Oh." Paul cracked his knuckles.

The screen door opened. "Here you are! I put chocolate fudge and whipped cream on top of the ice cream. I've got nuts, too, if you want them—chopped almonds, peanuts, walnuts fresh from the shell." Aunt Zona swooped down on us with the plates.

"Oh, no thanks, Mrs. Crenshaw. This is fine."

"Aunt Zona. All of Billy Lou's friends call me Aunt Zona."

Nobody ever called Aunt Zona "Aunt Zona" except me.

Paul munched about as fast as he could. I kept glaring at Aunt Zona, hoping she'd take the hint and go inside.

"Now let's get acquainted," Aunt Zona said. "Tell me all about yourself, Paul. Where do you go to Sunday School?"

Inside the house, the phone rang. I held my breath.

After the third ring, Aunt Zona said, "I guess I'd better get that." She rushed into the house.

"I've got to go pretty soon," Paul said. "I've got lots of homework. All those subjects and predicates to underline."

"I did that at school. Tonight I've got to finish something extra I'm writing for Mr. Forster."

"Something extra? What?"

I hesitated. I couldn't tell Paul about taking the manila paper, and about my make-up assignment. I shrugged and said, "I decided to write an adventure story. It's about the marvelous Mr. Mystifaction."

"Who?"

"He's a superhero, like Green Lantern and Superman. Only he gets out of trouble by using his mysterious mystifacting powers."

"That sounds good."

"Right now I've got him locked in a closet with a ticking bomb," I said.

"Oo. What happens next?"

"I don't know. I think I'm going to have to write another chapter. Maybe a whole book." I'd never thought of this before, but somehow saying it to Paul made it sound right. In my excitement, I put my hand down in my whipped cream.

While I was licking my hand off, Paul said, "Look. If you're going to write a whole book, you'll need an illustrator."

"I guess so." I'd never thought of that, either.

"Why don't I do the pictures and you do the writing? I'm an artist. I mean, I like to draw, and I've got a whole box of colored pencils. Mr. Forster would probably like it. He might give us both extra credit if we did a whole book."

I stood up on the steps and hopped from one foot to the other. "And we could make a fancy cover. And staple it. Only I've got to think of a second chapter."

Paul set his plate on the steps and headed for his bike. "Bring me the first chapter tomorrow, and I'll do the pictures for it."

"Okay, I will!" I was still on the steps, thinking about my book, when Aunt Zona came back out.

"Your friend gone already?" Aunt Zona picked up the plates. "Quit your jiggling, Billy Lou. The neighbors will think you've got St. Vitus' Dance."

"I'm writing a book, Aunt Zona!" I shouted. "And Paul's doing the pictures."

"I could write a book," Aunt Zona said as we went into the house. "My life story. All about me and your Uncle Emmett, and our little confectionary parlor in Armourdale before the '51 flood washed us out. Call it *Sweets and the Not So Sweet*. Some of those poor, down-and-out customers we had during the Depression. Hooo-eee, the smell! How about writing my book for me, Billy Lou? I'll let you be my ghost writer. Pay you a nickel a page."

"Well . . ." Aunt Zona's story didn't sound as interesting as mine. "Maybe after I finish this book."

"That Bennett Cerf on 'What's My Line' would pay us a thousand dollars to publish it, I'll bet."

All the time she was fixing supper, Aunt Zona talked about her life story. But I didn't really listen. I sat at the kitchen table and wrote in my Big Chief tablet:

Pow! The bomb exploded! But the marvelous
Mr. Mystifaction walked out of the closet
without a scratch!

I sat and thought about how he did it.

As soon as I walked into the room the next morning, I put Chapter 1 on Paul's desk. Then I hurried to the blackboard with *Bartlett's Familiar Quotations.* It was my turn to put up the Thought for the Day. I'd have to pick one on the spot. Last night I'd been too busy writing to think about famous quotations.

While I was leafing through *Bartlett's,* Paul came in and picked up the chapter. He sat down to read it before he even took his jacket off. I couldn't stop watching him read. In fact, I forgot all about choosing my Thought. When the tardy bell rang, I quickly started turning *Bartlett's* pages again.

Paul took out his colored pencil set while I was writing on the board.

Thought for the Day
While there's life there's hope.
Miguel de Cervantes.

During arithmetic Paul passed me the first finished picture. The marvelous Mr. Mystifaction had turned his body into a gigantic baseball bat. He was knocking the exploding bomb out of the locked closet.

"That's great!" I shouted.

Everyone turned and looked at me. Mr. Forster raised an eyebrow. "I never realized long division was so much fun, Louis," he said mildly.

I shoved the picture under my notebook and went

back to work. But when Mr. Forster wasn't looking, I flashed Paul the OK sign.

As we were walking out to the playground at recess, I said, "I'll start Chapter 2 during lunch."

Paul said, "What we really need now is a low-down, dirty, sneaky, underhanded, double-crossing ratfink of a villain."

Paul stood next to me in the dugout, and we kept on talking. For once, I didn't notice my turn at bat was coming until Robert Goldsmith, who was pitching for the other team, yelled, "Shake it up, Billy Lou! Move those buns!"

How could I have let this happen? I grimaced at Paul. It was all his fault. If he hadn't kept me so busy talking, I could have managed to slip to the end of the line again. Now I would actually have to take my turn. Strike out. Have Mickey Blake and the other guys on my team yell at me.

"Go on, Louis," Paul whispered. "Show them what we practiced last night. You can do it."

Another out. Billy Lou Lamb was going to make another out. Might as well get it over with.

Robert's team called out at me as I walked to the plate. "Attababy, Billy Lou. Slugger boy. Swing that bat!" Everyone on Robert's team moved in about six feet closer. Robert had to make some of them go back—they were getting in front of the pitcher's mark.

I choked up the way Mr. Forster had showed me. Where was Mr. Forster? Was he watching this? I couldn't see him.

Robert wound up and pitched. I let the ball go by.

"Strike!" Ricky Culligan shouted. He was umpire today because Frankie Burns was sick and the teams were uneven. Someone was nearly always sick. When the teams were even, Mr. Forster had to umpire.

"That's okay, Billy Lou," Mickey Blake called. "Let 'em go by. Goldsmith can't pitch—he'll walk you."

"Eat it, Blake!" Robert Goldsmith snapped. He let another ball go. It almost hit me.

"Ball one!" Ricky cried.

"Choke up some more," Paul yelled.

I choked up some more. Another ball came by. I don't know why, but something made me want to swing at it.

"Strike two!" Ricky did a little tap dance. Mickey Blake slapped the side of his own head.

"Here comes another one," Robert said.

"Swing!" called someone on Robert's team.

I swung again, clutching the bat so hard that my knuckles turned dead white.

Crack. The ball made a long arc into the air, right over the heads of all the fielders who were crowding around the pitcher.

Nobody moved.

"RUN, BILLY LOU!" Everyone on my team shouted at once. "RUN, BABY, RUN!"

Somehow I got my feet to run. I dropped the bat. The other team still wasn't moving. They were all staring at the ball as it flew higher and higher. I rounded first. Some of the fielders began to stir. The left fielder started to run back.

The ball dropped over the fence. By Miss Cobb's special rule, an automatic out.

I stopped running. So that was that. Another out for Billy Lou. The most spectacular out yet. I walked slowly toward the dugout.

At the exact same moment, all the guys on both teams broke out in a long, loud cheer. My own team was jumping up and down and clapping. Even Mickey Blake looked happy.

"You did it, Billy Lou. You finally got a hit. Way to go, Billy Lou," Mickey said.

A couple of guys slapped me on the back, hard.

"Next time, it'll be a home run," Mickey said. "You'll even have a batting average. What a slugger!"

I stopped dead. Everyone was smiling at me and carrying on. They'd never treated me like this before. I ought to feel happy.

"Stop saying that!" The words suddenly burst into the air, from nowhere. It wasn't until a minute or so later that I recognized the sound of my own voice, yelling. "Just stop it! I didn't get a hit. I didn't score any run. I knocked the stupid ball over the fence. I made an out. And you know what? I did it on purpose!"

I kept on yelling, but somewhere along the line I stopped listening to what I was saying. It was as if a switch had turned off. I knew I was still screaming, but for me, it was just a peaceful fall morning, and someone was burning trash down the street. I could smell the smoke. Then Mr. Forster came running up behind

54

me and put his arm around my shoulders, and I could feel that I was shaking.

"What happened?" Mr. Forster asked.

Mickey told him. Nobody else was talking. They were all just looking at me.

Mr. Forster squeezed my shoulder. "Go inside and clean up," he told me. "When you feel better, come back to class. There's no hurry."

I wiped my nose on my sleeve.

Paul's face caught my eye. I don't think I've ever seen anyone look so disgusted. "God, Louis," he said, and turned away.

I don't remember anything else that happened that day, except that when I got home from school I went straight to my room and took the china unicorn off my dresser. I held it up to the window so that the sun hit it just right, and the unicorn's horn started to glow. Then I put all the animals on the floor in a circle. I stood in the center of the circle, and I made the animals dance.

♥

6

The good thing about softball is that kickball season starts in mid-October. If I could just hide out for three weeks, I wouldn't have to play softball again until spring. Maybe before that I could convince Aunt Zona to move us back to Armourdale, Kansas, or to Alaska.

There was a good place at the east end of the playground, on the steps that led up to the kindergarten room. I could crouch down on the fourth or fifth step, and the stone wall in front of the steps would cover me. If I was the first one out of class at recess time, I could be in my hiding place before the other guys got out of the bathroom.

It worked for a day. I escaped from morning and afternoon recess, both. Mr. Forster didn't have playground duty that week. Even if my team noticed I didn't make it out to recess, nobody told Mr. Forster. I was free. The trouble was, I couldn't take a book out with me, because Mr. Forster would notice it. I couldn't raise my head over the wall to watch the games on the playground. Someone might see me. So there was nothing to do in my hiding place, except trace my fingers along the cracks in the stone wall.

By my second morning of hiding, I was going crazy. I didn't feel free anymore. I just felt bored and lonely. I missed Paul. My only friend. Finally I started to sing to myself, my own versions of songs I'd heard on Radio 71-derful WHB. I sang *To know, know, know me is to love, love, love me* a little too loud. A kindergarten girl came down the steps and said, "Don't you know this is nap time? Be quiet!"

Right away Miss Rosenthal, the kindergarten teacher, who was about ninety-two and walked like she was made of a thousand steel springs, appeared out of nowhere and grabbed my collar.

Miss Rosenthal propelled me to the sixth-grade play area and said, "Billy Lou Lamb, you're a big boy. Life is real, life is earnest. You can't sit on the kindergarten steps forever." She set me in the painted dugout in front of everyone and then left.

My team smirked at me, but nobody said anything. Especially Paul didn't say anything.

Now I would have to play out the rest of the season. Twenty-seven more recesses. I found out that if you hold your neck at just the right angle, you can look right past people's faces and see nothing but sky, and still be able to keep your balance when you walk and not run into things. Very often.

The thing is, there's really no way to shut your ears off, unless you keep your fingers in them all the time. You can hear people talk, and you can hear people not talk to you. Like Paul. Even in class, he never whispered to me. He never borrowed my English papers or asked the answer to an arithmetic problem. He talked to Robert Goldsmith, though. He even walked home from school with Robert. Twice.

I kept on writing the book about Mr. Mystifaction, but there were no more illustrations. It wasn't as much fun. I finally ended the story after Mr. Mystifaction conquered the Thing That Ate the Liberty Memorial in Chapter 6. Then I stapled a plain blue construction-paper cover on the pages. I thought of something good to do with Paul's picture. I copied a word from one of my books at home onto the bottom of it. *Frontispiece.* Then I pasted the picture to the inside front cover. That made it look as if there were supposed to be only one illustration.

I also put Paul's name on the title page.

MISCELLANEOUS ADVENTURES OF
THE MARVELOUS MR. MYSTIFACTION
by W. Louis Lamb
with
Illustration by Paul Harte
copyright © 1958 by W. L. Lamb

I didn't actually plan to copy the book, but that last line sort of made it official, like a library book.

One morning just before class I left the book on Mr. Forster's desk. Mr. Forster picked it up and flipped through the pages once. Then he smiled and put the book down again without saying anything.

The next day at English time, Mr. Forster said to the class, "Before we open our books today, I have a special treat for you. One of your classmates is an author." He held up *Miscellaneous Adventures of the Marvelous Mr. Mystifaction.* "I have to confess this is the best book I've read in a long time. Louis, I wonder if you'd mind reading your story to the class."

A lot of heads turned to look at me. Not Paul's, though.

My feet seemed to be melting. They ran through the soles of my shoes and stuck to the floor. I almost didn't get up. But then I thought, it's not about me. The story is about the marvelous Mr. Mystifaction. And anyway, I've got nothing to lose now. So I walked to Mr. Forster. I wiped my hands on my pants and took the book.

The first thing I did was show Paul's illustration to the class. "This is the marvelous Mr. Mystifaction, drawn by Paul Harte," I announced. I turned around slowly so that everyone in the room could see the picture. Out of the corner of my eye, I saw Paul blush. But he didn't look mad.

Veronica Allison said, "I just admire artistic men so much."

Mr. Forster flashed Veronica a "don't interrupt" look.

I began: "At the farthest reaches of the galaxy lies the planet Archon, home of an incredible race of supermagicians. The greatest of them all is known on Earth as the marvelous Mr. Mystifaction—master of transformations, befuddler of crooks, spies, and villains."

It took me almost the whole English period to read all six chapters aloud. Nobody minded that. In fact, everyone paid better attention to me than they usually did to Mr. Forster. My voice seemed to get stronger and clearer as I went along. I sounded more like the marvelous Mr. Mystifaction and less like me.

After I read the last sentence, a few people clapped. When Mr. Forster didn't say anything, more kids joined in. Finally almost everyone in the room was clapping. Somehow, this clapping felt different to me than those cheers on the playground. Somehow this time I couldn't stop grinning.

Then Mickey Blake started to whistle through his teeth, and Mr. Forster cleared his throat. "I think that's enough appreciation, although I must agree, Louis has earned it. Maybe now some of the rest of you will feel like trying your hands at a story, too."

That got him onto paragraphs and complete sentences, and the fun was over.

Later that morning I thought I saw Paul glance at me. But by the time I looked back, he was busy with something in his desk.

When the noon dismissal bell rang, Mr. Forster stopped me at the door. "If you don't mind waiting a minute, Louis, I'd like to talk to you." The rest of the class went off to lunch.

Mr. Forster opened the top drawer of his desk. He pulled out a notebook. Not a school notebook, but one without spirals or rings. It had a black cardboard cover that was speckled like marble, and it was stitched up the side like a real book. Mr. Forster handed it to me. "I meant what I said about your story, Louis. It *is* good. I think there might be a real writer in you."

I started to say thank you, but Mr. Forster went on.

"My best friend is a writer, and he says the way he got started was by keeping a journal. He says that writing about what happened to him helped him understand other people better, and then he could write about them, too. Maybe you're not interested in being a writer right now. But if you ever are, you can use this notebook for your journal. I mean, your *first* journal."

This time the "thank you" wouldn't come out. I found myself staring at Mr. Forster's wristwatch. His wrist was covered with blond hairs that gleamed in the sunlight coming in from the windows behind us.

"I guess we'd better get to our lunches before we both starve to death," Mr. Forster said.

I went home to have lunch with Aunt Zona. All along the way, I ran my hands up and down the smooth surface of the cover that looked like black marble. I tried to think of something to write in my journal. Whatever it would be, it would have to be something important.

I got back to school five minutes before the afternoon tardy bell. A few kids were already at their desks. Paul was there, reading his library book. He half looked up when I sat down next to him.

61

I took out my arithmetic book and yesterday's homework. I started to check some thought problems.

Veronica Allison walked by Paul's desk, twirling some pompons she wore on a velvet cord around her neck. "My parents can't pick me up after school today," she said to the air, "so I guess I'll have to walk home alone. Unless, of course, someone offers to keep me company." Veronica paused, still twirling.

Paul said nothing.

The bell rang. A few minutes later a piece of folded-up tablet paper landed on my desk. I opened it up and read:

Louis can you walk home from school today? Paul

I got my red pencil out. On the back of the note I wrote in huge letters:

SURE

All that softball practice must have paid off after all. When I tossed the note back to Paul, it landed exactly in the middle of page 87 of his arithmetic book.

I could hardly wait for the afternoon to end.

About fifteen minutes before time to go home, the inside door swung open suddenly. Miss Cobb came into the room at a tilt, as if a high wind were blowing behind her. She was carrying a thick stack of pink papers with purple writing on them. Miss Cobb came to a stop by Mr. Forster's desk.

"Excuse me, Mr. Forster and boys and girls," she

said. "I have an important announcement to make." Miss Cobb fixed the class with a stare that lasted until everyone had put down pencils and papers. "As you all know, in three weeks Alcott School will be having its annual Open House." A few kids groaned. Miss Cobb's eyes made a quick, fierce sweep of the room. The groans stopped.

"This year I hope we'll have perfect attendance on Open House night. I'd just love to visit with each and every one of your parents, and so would Mr. Forster." Miss Cobb began to pass the pink papers around. "Now boys and girls, I want each of you to take one of these home with you tonight."

The papers turned out to be invitations.

At the top, someone had drawn a woman with a large head and a tiny body standing by a house with an open door. The woman was supposed to be Louisa May Alcott. You could tell that because it said so right under her feet. Below was printed:

COME ONE!!! COME ALL!!!!
TO LOUISA MAY ALCOTT ELEMENTARY
SCHOOL'S ANNUAL OPEN HOUSE
THURSDAY, OCTOBER 23, 1958
7:00 P.M. TO 9:30 P.M.
PROGRAM IN AUDITORIUM FIRST.
HEAR THE REVEREND FLOYD HARDCASTLE
SPEAK ON "THE MENACE IN OUR PUBLIC SCHOOLS"
THEN VISIT YOUR CHILD'S TEACHER
AND CLASSROOM.
GRANDPARENTS AND OTHERS WELCOME.

Veronica Allison held up an index card. It read:

I WONDER WHO'S GOING TO BE
MY DATE FOR OPEN HOUSE.

"I've got lots more invitations in my office for your neighbors and uncles and aunts," Miss Cobb told us. "All you have to do is ask." Miss Cobb nodded to Mr. Forster. Then she left the room as fast as she had come in.

Another folded-up piece of tablet paper fell on my desk. This one said:

Veronica Allison is the menace in our public schools.

On it Paul had drawn a picture of a roly-poly girl dressed in tight black clothes that were all too small. The girl had eyelashes about a foot long and fat, fat lips colored neon red. And only one snaggly tooth.

"Pass it to Veronica," Paul whispered to me.

I wrote Veronica's name on the note and passed it on.

Mr. Forster said, "I'm really looking forward to meeting all of your families." He went on for a while about putting our best work out for Open House being like putting our best foot forward.

Veronica Allison let out a sharp scream. She fanned Paul's note up and down, her eyes round and wide. At first she looked as if she might be blinking back tears, then her face settled into a scowl. "Paul Harte," she shouted, "this is slander! You wait. You just wait."

The dismissal bell went off. You could hear Veronica carry on right over it. Somewhere through the noise Mr. Forster was saying, "... and don't forget to take your invitations with you. ..."

Paul and I snatched up our things and made a dash for the door, but Veronica was right behind us. She chased us for five blocks before we cut through someone's back yard and lost her.

I can say one good thing for Veronica Allison. She could run pretty fast in those black dancing slippers.

7

"Hold still, Billy Lou," Aunt Zona said again. It was the third time she'd tried to fix my tie since we'd left for Open House. Somehow when I tied it, the long skinny part of the tie always dangled two inches below the thick part. Aunt Zona's tying was worse. She pulled the knot right up to my Adam's apple. Almost cut off my oxygen.

Aunt Zona stood back on the school steps and brushed invisible somethings off the shoulders of my navy blue suit. Parents and kids in their best clothes walked by us. They all looked like strangers impersonating themselves.

Aunt Zona gave my suit a final flick. We went into the building and headed for the auditorium. Aunt Zona walked faster than I did. Clouds of the perfume she had bought last week from the Fuller Brush man trailed after her. I hoped some unsuspecting family didn't walk in the door behind us and get all that Fuller Brush smell smack in the face.

The walls were covered with posters that said things like "WELCOME PARENTS" and "LOUISA MAY ALCOTT SAYS, 'MY HOUSE IS YOUR HOUSE.'"

Claudia Hardcastle's parents stood at the back door of the auditorium. Mrs. Hardcastle's wig shone blue under the hall lights. "Oh, there's Brother Hardcastle," Aunt Zona said. She tugged at her pink dress.

"We're all looking forward to your talk, Brother Hardcastle," Aunt Zona said. She clasped Reverend Hardcastle's hand with both of hers. I didn't see how Aunt Zona could do that. Reverend Hardcastle's hands were long and white and moist. I always hated to touch them when he tried to shake hands with me after church services.

Tonight he only squeezed my shoulder. "Good to see you, son," Reverend Hardcastle said. He left a damp spot on my suit.

"Floyd's been practicing all day," Mrs. Hardcastle told us. "He gets so nervous when he has to speak outside of church. 'Floyd,' I say to him, 'it's all the Lord's work, doesn't matter a bit where you do it.' But he's just so anxious to do a good job."

"Well, a little Milk of Magnesia always makes *me* feel bright as a penny," Aunt Zona said. Her voice carried over the other conversations around us. "That's what I always tell Billy Lou. Don't I, Billy Lou?"

"Maybe we better sit down, Aunt Zona. It's getting pretty crowded." I started walking into the auditorium.

"Goodness sake, Billy Lou, just hold your horses." Aunt Zona told the Hardcastles she would see them later. "What's your hurry?" she said, as she caught up

67

with me. "They can't start without Brother Hardcastle, you know."

Aunt Zona aimed us for two seats on the aisle, seven or eight rows from the front. We sat down. Aunt Zona arranged herself in her seat a couple of times.

Someone tapped my shoulder from behind. Paul.

"Where'd you come from?" I said.

"Where'd *you* come from?" Paul said. Then he pointed to the people sitting next to him. "Louis, these are my parents, Mr. and Mrs. Harte, and my sister, Beth."

I started to say hello. Then I saw Paul's sister. Beth Harte had hearing aids in both ears. On top of that, she wore huge, thick glasses that made her eyes seem to float out at you like something from a 3-D movie.

Paul made quick motions with his fingers. Beth gave a kind of silent giggle and flashed her own fingers back at Paul.

I tried not to stare.

Paul was introducing his parents to Aunt Zona.

If you ignored the hearing aids and the glasses, you could see that Beth Harte looked something like Paul. Without them, she would have been pretty. She had long, shiny blonde hair. She smiled at me, and I smiled back, trying to think of what to say. I didn't know any sign language.

The auditorium lights began to flicker. People who had been standing in the aisles hurried to seats.

Miss Cobb appeared on stage. Reverend and Mrs. Hardcastle walked on behind her and stood by folding chairs next to the podium. Somewhere backstage, someone blew on a trumpet. Miss Cobb and the Hardcastles looked respectful. Gradually, everyone in the auditorium stood up. The trumpet turned out to be playing "The Star Spangled Banner."

A couple of Cub Scouts came out of the wings carrying the Missouri and U.S. flags. We waited while they fixed them in the flag holders on either side of the stage. The Scout carrying the Missouri flag was having trouble. The trumpet finished playing and he still hadn't got the flag to stay put.

A man came onstage to help him. It was Mr. Forster, wearing a dark brown suit I'd never seen before. The two of them worked on the flag holder a while. Finally Mr. Forster gave up, and the Scout walked offstage with him. The Missouri flag stayed at a funny tilt, as if there had just been a small earthquake that left it that way.

Miss Cobb didn't look at it. She said, "Good evening, faculty, parents, students, and friends. And welcome to Louisa May Alcott School's annual Open House. Before you leave this evening, I hope to have the chance to speak with every single one of you." There must have been a thousand people in the room. I didn't see how Miss Cobb was going to get around to every single one of us.

Miss Cobb said, "As everyone knows, these are times of great challenge for our public schools. Everywhere we look, there are challenges. Great and small. As an educator, I feel privileged to live in these challenging times. Tonight we are lucky enough to have with us one of our community leaders, the Reverend Floyd Hardcastle, minister of the New Jerusalem Baptist Church."

Mrs. Hardcastle muttered something to her.

"*And* chaplain of the Midtown V.F.W. Reverend Hardcastle will say a few words on the problems and challenges we face in our schools. Reverend Hardcastle."

Everyone applauded.

Reverend Hardcastle stepped up to the podium. He took a sheaf of crumpled notebook paper from inside his suit coat. At first I could hardly hear him. I wondered what Beth Harte was thinking, and if she understood anything that was going on. Probably she could read lips. I tried it, but I couldn't read Reverend Hardcastle's very well. He was saying something about walking five miles to school every morning and five miles back every night when he was a boy in Odessa, Missouri.

After a few minutes, Reverend Hardcastle picked up steam. He began to get louder, the way he did on Sunday mornings at church. He told us that the good old days were over. Aunt Zona's elbow poked me. "That's sure the truth," she said. Someone went "ssshh."

Reverend Hardcastle said that the enemies of American liberty were everywhere. Even in the public schools. He said that only last year a teacher in Kansas City was fired for being a member of the Communist Party.

70

The room got very still.

Reverend Hardcastle shuffled his papers for a moment. Then he went on. He talked about all the juvenile delinquents standing outside Paseo High School smoking cigarettes every afternoon and no one being able to lift a finger to stop them. He said a lot of other things, but I began to think about Beth Harte again, so I missed most of them.

What would it be like to have a deaf sister? I wanted to turn my head and look at her again, but I couldn't. Paul's parents looked nice. They were younger than Aunt Zona, but Mrs. Harte had a little gray in her hair.

When I tuned back in on Reverend Hardcastle, he was just about finished. He said that the public schools were the cornerstone of democracy. And he said that teenagers should not be allowed to smoke cigarettes right in front of a high school. Then he sat down.

The audience clapped politely.

Miss Cobb said, "Thank you, Reverend Hardcastle. And now we'll adjourn so that you parents can meet with your children's teachers."

Right away the aisles of the auditorium were flooded with people.

Aunt Zona and I walked out with the Hartes. Aunt Zona shouted at Beth. She asked her how she liked Kansas City. She asked it three or four times.

"I didn't know you had a deaf sister—I mean, a sister," I whispered to Paul.

"Yeah," Paul said. "One of the reasons we moved to

Kansas City is because there are good schools here for Beth."

"Could you teach me some sign language?" I asked.

"Sure. It's easy." Paul made some words with his fingers. I was sorry Beth Harte was deaf, but in a way I envied Paul and Beth. Sign language looked like fun.

Mr. Forster was standing in the doorway of Room 3.

Aunt Zona shook his hand. "It sure is nice to meet Billy Lou's teacher," she said.

Mr. Forster said, "The pleasure is mutual, Mrs. Crenshaw. You have a very talented nephew. You've read his book, I hope. It's on the bulletin board tonight where everyone can see it."

"Talent runs in the family," Aunt Zona said. "Billy Lou's mother was a tap dancer."

"Is that right?"

"If Billy Lou ever gives you any trouble, Mr. Foster, you just send him right home and I'll give him a good licking." Aunt Zona chuckled.

"Forster," Mr. Forster said. "My name is Forster." He smiled and turned to Paul's parents.

We walked into the classroom.

Mr. Forster had done a great job of decorating. The walls were covered with baked clay masks we had made in art class. There was a colored folder of homework papers on every kid's desk. My book was in the center of the bulletin board, just like Mr. Forster said. It was opened to the first page of Chapter 1. Some of the other kids' self-portraits were arranged in a ring around the book, so that the book looked extra important.

"Here comes that Veronica Allison," Aunt Zona said. "Wearing lipstick. Wouldn't you know it."

Veronica was also wearing her hair in a French twist. She had on a peasant blouse with a scoop neck and red high-heeled shoes.

"I don't know what those Allisons can be thinking of, letting that kid get all gussied up like a gypsy," Aunt Zona said, loud enough for Veronica to hear.

Veronica and her parents were talking to Mr. Forster. Her father's face was flushed, and he kept mopping his forehead. Mrs. Allison looked tired. Her heels were lower than Veronica's.

Reverend and Mrs. Hardcastle came in right behind the Allisons, with Claudia in tow.

The Hardcastles spotted Aunt Zona. "Well, what do you think of this new teacher?" Mrs. Hardcastle said to Aunt Zona. "I suppose you know he's having the children read books about evolution."

"I think it's real nice for Billy Lou to have a man teacher," Aunt Zona said.

"Oh, yes. I didn't say it wasn't." Mrs. Hardcastle made a swipe at her wig. "Even so. Some things make you wonder."

Reverend Hardcastle stood behind her, looking sad and serious but not saying a word.

Mrs. Hardcastle went on. "I tell Floyd, it's all well and good to worry about Communists and juvenile delinquents, but where do you think children get those ideas? I mean, it just stands to reason, if the adults are permissive. It all has to start somewhere. Not that Mr.

Forster isn't a good teacher. I'm sure he's a very fine teacher, of course."

I tried to steer Aunt Zona away, but Mrs. Hardcastle had her pinned. While they were talking, I noticed Ellie Siegel and her parents. Ellie had finally taken the bandage off her leg. Mrs. Siegel was flipping through the papers on Ellie's desk and frowning. Mr. Siegel seemed younger than Mrs. Siegel—kind of nice, really. He didn't look to me like someone who could be Ellie's father. Ellie held on to one of his hands while her mother flipped through papers.

It was funny to see all these kids with their parents. Sometimes the kids looked just like their parents, and the family fit neatly together like a set of paper dolls. But most of the time the kids and parents didn't fit together at all. Take Mickey Blake. Mickey was thin and wiry, with slick dark hair, but his mother must have weighed about two hundred pounds. She had brown hair pulled back in a pony tail and tied with a rubber band, and she wore black and white saddle oxfords. She looked more like a very fat babysitter than somebody's mother. On the other hand, some of the parents looked old enough to be grandparents. Both of Georgia Smith's parents had white hair.

Paul tapped me on the shoulder. Robert Goldsmith was with him. Robert gave me half a smile. I gave half a smile back.

"Let's go outside for a while," Paul said. "It's stuffy in here."

"There's not enough oxygen in this room for the

number of persons," Robert said. "Any minute now people will start to hyperventilate." Robert looked as if he might enjoy staying to watch this, but he headed for the outside door with Paul and me.

The night air was crisp and cool. It was the kind of night when the stars look so bright, they almost hurt your eyes. The only sound was the occasional dry clack of leaves against the fence when a small breeze hit them.

For no reason, Paul started running around the schoolyard in circles. Robert began to run, too. I watched from the stoop and wondered if I was supposed to join them. Then I decided it didn't matter what I was supposed to do. I wanted to run. So I did. My tie flapped against my chest. It felt good to be running for no reason. Not like a race. Like fun.

Veronica Allison and Claudia Hardcastle came out together and stood in front of the door.

Paul and Robert and I ran right by them. Again and again we ran by, until my side began to hurt and all three of us were gasping. Finally we collapsed on the stoop next to the girls.

"It's really nice out here," Claudia said.

"The night was made for love," Veronica said. She started humming.

We just looked at them.

"I guess we better go back inside," Paul said at last.

"Yeah," Robert said.

But we sat there a while longer.

I don't know how much time went by, but at last the

door opened and Paul's mother stuck her head out. "Shake a leg, kiddo," she said. "We've been looking all over for you. It's time to go home. Tomorrow's a school day."

So then the rest of us had to go inside and find our families, too.

The place was clearing out fast. Only a few parents and kids were still milling around. Mrs. Blake and Mickey were talking to the Hardcastles. The Allisons were pulling on their coats. Next to the teacher's desk, Mrs. Siegel was shaking her finger at Mr. Forster. "... Ellie is a delicate child. A sensitive child," she was saying. "Not that I want you to baby the girl, Mr. Forster, I certainly don't baby her at home, I'm a strict mother, you can ask anyone, but as I've told you before, Ellie just can't be forced..." I edged by them as quickly as I could.

Aunt Zona was reading through the papers on my desk. As I was walking toward her, the inside door of the classroom opened and a man started to come in. He got just past the threshold and said, "Jack—"

Then he stopped short. He looked like he was counting the people in the room. "Oh, I'm early," he said, turning red. "I didn't mean to—I'll—sorry." He spun around and disappeared out the door.

Mr. Forster turned a little red, too.

Mrs. Siegel noticed that right away. "Anything wrong, Mr. Forster? I hope we're not keeping you from something important."

Mr. Forster cleared his throat. He started winding

his wristwatch. "Oh, no. That was just my ride home." Mr. Forster kept winding, without looking at the watch face.

Mrs. Hardcastle poked Mrs. Blake in the elbow. They began to amble toward the outside door.

"Well, everyone." Mr. Forster's voice sounded phony-cheerful. "I suppose we'd better break up the party." He finally looked down at his watch. "It's nearly ten."

Aunt Zona said, "Early to bed, early to rise, makes a man healthy, wealthy, and wise. Come on, Billy Lou."

I wanted to hang around and see if the strange man would come back and what Mr. Forster would say then. But Aunt Zona had a strong grip. I barely had time to call "Good night!" to Paul and the Hartes before she had me out on the stoop.

Mrs. Hardcastle and Mrs. Blake were standing in the schoolyard by themselves, talking in whispers. When Aunt Zona and I walked by, they looked up. "Oh, Mrs. Crenshaw," Mrs. Hardcastle said. "Lou Ellen and I were just wondering. This Mr. Forster. He's not married, is he?"

"Anyone could tell that," Aunt Zona hooted.

Mrs. Blake nodded at Mrs. Hardcastle.

Mrs. Hardcastle leaned toward Aunt Zona. "How do you mean?" she said.

"Why, if there was a Mrs. Foster, she'd have been right here tonight, serving cookies and punch. A person needs refreshment at these big do's. Men never think of things like that."

"Oh." Mrs. Hardcastle sounded disappointed.

"Matter of fact, that's what Billy Lou and I need right this minute. Soon as we get home, I'm going to fix us two nice chocolate sundaes." Aunt Zona propelled me out to the sidewalk, waving to Mrs. Hardcastle as we went.

Once I looked back and the Siegels had come outside with Ellie. Mrs. Hardcastle stopped them, too, but I couldn't hear what she was saying. Just then Aunt Zona gave me another tug, and by the time I turned around again, the schoolyard was out of sight.

8

Aunt Zona's skeletons were getting a little ragged around the edges. "Your Uncle Emmett bought these decorations in 1937," she told me. "Back when we still lived in Armourdale. We used to hang them in the store. Poor Emmett. I like to think he's watching us put them up tonight."

"What time is it now, Aunt Zona?"

"Five minutes later than it was last time you asked," Aunt Zona said. "Anyone'd think it was your first Halloween." She gave my cheek a friendly pinch.

It wasn't my first Halloween, but it would be the first Halloween I'd spent with my best friend. Halloween was on Friday this year, and Paul was coming over to spend the night. As a matter of fact, it would be the first time anyone had stayed over at our house.

Aunt Zona sniffed. "Lordy! That syrup's scorching!" She ran into the kitchen. Aunt Zona was making her popcorn balls for the trick-or-treaters. Paul and I would get one each.

I stood in the kitchen doorway and watched Aunt Zona tend the syrup. The air was hot and sweet. "Now this year," Aunt Zona said, stirring, "I don't want you to waste these good popcorn balls."

"I won't. *We* won't." Last year I'd forgotten all about the popcorn ball Aunt Zona gave me. One day around Thanksgiving she was mopping under my bed and out it rolled. I didn't think Aunt Zona was ever going to forgive me for that.

While Aunt Zona finished up the popcorn balls, I drifted back into the living room to inspect our work. There were cardboard skeletons hanging in all of the side windows and lighted plastic pumpkins in the front ones. Besides those, Aunt Zona had carved out a real jack o'lantern for the porch. I could see the back of it sitting on the low wall out front. Now that it was really dark, the glowing face would jump right out at the trick-or-treaters. And Paul, when he showed up.

Part of me wanted to go trick-or-treating, even though Aunt Zona said I should stay home and wait for my company. This would be the first year I'd ever missed. Of course, my old Superman costume was too small for me now, anyway. Aunt Zona was saving it for the church rummage sale.

Still no sign of Paul.

I decided to go back out to the kitchen and help Aunt Zona wrap popcorn balls. Every now and then, trick-or-treaters came to the door. Luckily, Aunt Zona had popped lots of corn.

Once I got up to go to the bathroom. When I came back to the kitchen, Aunt Zona had disappeared. I started to wrap more popcorn balls.

80

Just as I was cutting some waxed paper off the roll, a high, loud scream filled the air. It sounded like it was coming from our basement.

I couldn't move.

Aunt Zona was nowhere in sight. Maybe she'd gone to the basement for something and a burglar had got her.

"Aunt Zona?"

Another scream from the basement, a long, terrible one. Then the sound of feet climbing up the basement steps. Clump. Clump. Clump. Something scratched at the basement door, which happened to be right in the kitchen.

"Now what do you suppose that is?" Aunt Zona said from behind me. She scared me so much that I dropped the waxed paper, and it unrolled all over the kitchen floor.

The scratching noises stopped. The knob of the basement door turned slowly. It swung open.

A familiar figure with a green rubber face and sharp white fangs stood at the top of the basement steps.

"Frick or freat," Paul said through the fangs.

Aunt Zona howled, like he was the funniest thing she'd ever seen in her life.

I was a little mad. "You could cause a person heart failure," I told Paul. I bent over to roll up the waxed paper.

"Your aunt snuck me in while you were out of the room," Paul said, taking off the mask and fangs.

"You should have seen your expression, Billy Lou." Aunt Zona went off in another gale of laughter.

Paul put the fangs back in. He crossed his eyes and wiggled his ears until I laughed, too.

"You just make yourself right at home," Aunt Zona told Paul. "Have a popcorn ball." The doorbell rang, and she went off with an armload of small, round waxed-paper packages.

"It sure was dark in that basement," Paul said. "What kind of car do you have down there in the garage part?"

"Oh, that. My Uncle Emmett's 1940 Packard. It hasn't worked in years, but Aunt Zona doesn't want to get rid of it."

"Neat! Let's go down and look at it."

"With the light *on,*" I said, snapping the switch at the top of the steps. "Have you ever stayed up late on Halloween night before? At someone's house, I mean?" We walked down into the dimness.

"Sure," Paul said. "Oh, neat-o!" He ran his arm over the hood of Uncle Emmett's Packard. His arm came up black. Paul wiped it on his blue jeans.

"It's a little dirty," I said.

"But what a great old car!" Paul hopped up and down on the running board. The Packard barely creaked. "Let's get inside." Paul opened the door on the driver's side. We scrambled in. Paul got behind the wheel.

The smell of old car filled our nostrils. Inside, the Packard was almost as good as new. Uncle Emmett had believed in treating cars like animals. He used to

82

groom the Packard every week, inside and out. The tan-colored seats were still soft and plush and only a little sun-faded. They had some kind of ribbing on them, so that when you sank into them, parts of the seat pushed back at you.

Paul turned an imaginary key in the ignition, and we roared off. We raced Cadillacs, Chevvies, and one poor little Nash Rambler. Paul and I made a lot more noise than the Packard's real motor ever had, but we out-dragged everyone else on the highway. Paul brought us to a screeching stop back in the basement.

"Like on a dime," he crooned, and gave the dashboard a pat. "What else is down here?" Paul looked around as we got out.

"Lots of things. Junk, mostly."

"Hey, records!" Paul had found the old Victrola and my mother's stack of 78s. Some of them had been played almost white. "Does this thing work?"

"You have to plug it into the light socket," I said, reaching up.

We put up the lid of the Victrola and snapped the *on* switch. The Victrola whined a little, then the turntable started to spin. Not quite at full speed, but almost.

Paul picked out a record that wasn't too scratched up, and I put it on. The song was "Oh, Johnny, Oh, Johnny, Oh!" by someone called Wee Bonnie Baker.

Wee Bonnie sounded like she was about twelve years old. "She makes me think of Veronica Allison," I said.

"Eeeeuuu-ucchhh!" Paul clutched his stomach.

"Hey, I know what. Let's make creepy phone calls to people, like to Veronica."

"Well, I don't know." This didn't sound like something Aunt Zona would approve of.

"Oh, come on! It's Halloween! And Veronica deserves it. We'll pretend to be the Voice of Doom. We'll scare her out of her mind!"

"Well." I thought fast. "We could sneak the telephone into the hall closet. I think the cord will reach that far. That way, Aunt Zona won't hear us."

"So what are we waiting for? Let's do it!"

We closed up the Victrola and put Wee Bonnie back on the stack. Then we tiptoed up the basement steps.

I snapped off the light and opened the door to the kitchen as quietly as I could. No Aunt Zona. The TV was blaring in the living room. Aunt Zona must have set up camp in there with the rest of the popcorn balls.

It was easy to sneak the telephone off its perch in the dining room and into the hall closet. We had to push some coats and dresses aside, but there was really plenty of room for us to crouch down in there. We left the door open just enough that a crack of light came through.

Paul wanted to dial Veronica Allison first. Later, I wondered how come he knew her telephone number from memory, but at the time I was too busy thinking of what we would say.

Veronica's mother answered the phone. Paul asked for Veronica very politely, in his normal voice. But when Veronica came to the phone, Paul started to make eerie noises at the back of his throat. He pushed the receiver to me, and I joined in with a few moans and groans. Pretty good ones, I thought. I just pretended I had the flu and was going to throw up.

Then Paul said, in low, menacing tones, "This is the Voice of Doom. Beware. Beware."

He held the receiver close to my ear, so I could hear Veronica say, "Who is this?"

"The Voice . . . of . . . Doom," Paul repeated. "You must flee. Immediately. Get out of town before midnight tonight, or else."

"Or else what?" Veronica said. She didn't sound the least bit scared.

"Or else there will be worms in your girdle and bats in your blouse!" Paul banged down the receiver.

We sat still, savoring the thought of what was going to happen to Veronica if she didn't get out of town. "I don't think Veronica probably has a girdle," I said finally.

"It doesn't matter. It's the thought that counts."

"Who else shall we call?"

"How about Goldsmith?" Paul started to dial.

I shut my mouth tight. I wasn't sure I felt like scaring Robert Goldsmith. I didn't think Paul should be calling Robert from my closet. On the other hand, Paul was my guest. So I let him go ahead.

Robert answered the phone himself.

Paul started his Voice of Doom routine, but Robert cut in. He must have been expecting this type of thing. He said:

"Okay, Voice of Doom. Here's a poem for you.

"Ooey Gooey was a worm, a mighty worm was he.
One day upon the railroad tracks,
  a train he did not see.
Oo-ey Goo-ey!
And me without a spoon."

"God, Goldsmith!" Paul said, in his normal voice.

So after that we all talked for a few minutes. Robert said "Hi" to me. I decided maybe it had been a good idea to call Robert after all. Robert said he was home alone. His parents had gone to a party. Aunt Zona never let me stay by myself at night. In fact, Aunt Zona never went out at night. For a second I wished I were Robert.

Robert was waiting for Shock Theater to come on TV. He was going to watch "Son of Dracula."

"We could watch that," Paul said to me.

"Sure," I said.

Robert said, "You could write a Dracula book." I said I might, and we hung up.

"Now who?" I asked Paul.

"Ummmm. Mr. Forster! How about Mr. Forster?"

"Oh, come on." I giggled and slapped Paul on the elbow.

"No, I mean it."

"You can't call a *teacher* and pretend to be the Voice of Doom."

"Why not?" Paul said.

Somehow I couldn't think why not, but I knew you couldn't do it. After a minute, I said, "You'd get expelled. We both would."

86

"Only if we got caught. Anyway, you don't think Mr. Forster would really mind, do you? We wouldn't say what we said to Veronica, just something spooky and funny, like at the Halloween party at school."

Mr. Forster had let us tell ghost stories with the blinds drawn at the class party that afternoon. He even told one himself.

"We don't know Mr. Forster's telephone number," I said.

"So what? You've got a phone book, don't you?"

"It's in the dining room."

"Go get it."

"Yeah, but Aunt Zona—"

"God, Louis. Don't be so chicken!"

Of course, then I *had* to go get the phone book. I opened the closet door wide enough to sneak out. I could hear the TV blasting away at the front of the house. I tiptoed back to the dining room. The phone book was inside a cabinet near the alcove where the phone usually sat. I pulled it out just as Aunt Zona called, "Billy Lou? What are you boys doing?"

"Nothing, Aunt Zona," I shouted. "I'm going to show Paul my room."

"You want something to eat besides popcorn balls?"

"We're fine, Aunt Zona." Don't get up, Aunt Zona. Don't come in here now. I stood frozen in the middle of the dining room with the phone book under one arm. Aunt Zona didn't come in.

The TV sang, *"Sev-en-ty sev-en, Sun-set Strip. (Click. Click.)"*

I took fast giant steps into the hall closet. Crouching

87

in the narrow band of light, I flipped pages until I got to the *F*'s. *Forest. Fornelli. Fosdick.* No Forster.

"It isn't in here," I hissed.

"I guess it's too new to be listed," Paul said. "Wait a minute! Do you have that little blue directory the P.T.A. puts out?"

We did. Aunt Zona had stuck it inside the phone book in the *P*'s. I scanned it quickly. The directory gave the home addresses and phone numbers of all the teachers and room mothers. Mr. Forster's was on page 2.

Forster, Jack (Mr.)   7324 Arcadia   JAckson 2-8846

"All right!" Paul said. "You want to dial?"

"No, you do it." Something in my stomach rippled.

Paul picked up the receiver. He dialed Mr. Forster's number.

We bent our heads together to listen. One ring. Two rings. Three.

"He's probably not home. Let's hang up," I said.

Paul rolled his eyes and sighed at me.

On the fifth ring, someone answered. A man's voice said, "Hello?" It didn't sound to me like Mr. Forster.

"Hang up," I whispered to Paul. Then I pushed down the button in the phone cradle.

"Hey! What'd you do that for?"

"That wasn't Mr. Forster," I said. "It was probably the wrong number. You would have been doing the Voice of Doom for a total stranger."

Paul looked exasperated. "Okay. You dial." He shoved the phone at me.

I dialed. J . . . A . . . 2 . . . 8 . . . 8 . . . 4 . . . 6. Every digit was right this time. I was sure of it. My stomach did that rippling thing again.

Mr. Forster's line rang twice. Then the voice. "Hello?"

"It's the same person," I mouthed at Paul.

But Paul went ahead. "Good evening," he said, sounding like Alfred Hitchcock. "This is the Voice of Doom."

"What?" the man on the phone said sharply.

"This-s-s is the Voice of Doom."

For a minute there was no sound at all on the other end of the line. Then the voice again, mad: "What is this? Who are you?"

Paul's Voice of Doom got a little quavery, but he went on. "You must beware. Be-e-ware."

The voice at Mr. Forster's end drifted away, as if it was talking to someone in another room. I heard it say, "Jack."

I motioned at Paul to hang up. Paul started to.

Then the man's voice came on again, loud. "I don't know who you are and how you got this number, but I advise you not to call here again. The police—"

There was an interruption. Voices muttering out of range of the phone.

I couldn't stand it. I grabbed the receiver and banged it down, hard. Two times, to be sure.

Paul let out a shaky laugh. "Boy. He sure sounded mad. I mean, he acted like it was some kind of crime. Not just a Halloween joke."

"Maybe we better not call anyone else tonight," I said.

"I guess not," Paul said. "Anyway, it must be almost time for Shock Theater."

I didn't answer. I was thinking. Who was that man on Mr. Forster's phone? A brother? Mr. Forster's father, maybe? No, his family lived in Virginia. Whoever it was, I felt sorry for Mr. Forster if his friends were all that touchy. Would the man really have called the police?

"We better put the phone back," Paul said.

"Yeah."

But the whole time we were sneaking the phone and the phone book back into the dining room, I was listening for sirens. I half expected a black-and-white car to pull up in front of the house. I knew that man on the phone had no way of tracing us. But still . . .

"Snap out of it, Louis. It's time for the movie." Paul grabbed my shoulder and shook it lightly.

I let Paul push me into the living room, where Aunt Zona was just gathering up the last of her popcorn balls. Creepy organ music was coming out of the TV set.

Aunt Zona clucked at the TV. "I don't see how you boys can watch all that scary stuff. I'm going to bed, myself." Aunt Zona gave me a poke on her way out of the room. "Don't let anything get you tonight, Billy Lou," she said.

I forced a smile and tried my best to concentrate on "Son of Dracula." But I couldn't stop shivering.

9

On the day I got in trouble at school, we were making bottle people. Miss Cobb had come up with the idea. Each class was to bring in old bottles from home and decorate them as people. The best bottle people would go in the All-City Art Fair.

I had one of Aunt Zona's hand lotion bottles, and there wasn't much I could do with it. I finally decided to make it into a cleaning lady. The cap looked like an upside down bucket. All I had to do was take it off and paint it gray. Then I added a couple of pipe cleaner arms, a papier mâché head, and a little yarn for hair.

"She looks just like the woman who used to clean the cafeteria at the Academy in Alexandria," Mr. Forster told me. He beamed me one of his most encouraging smiles. Those were the smiles he usually saved up for people like Ellie Siegel, so I knew how crummy my bottle lady really looked.

Mr. Forster was getting plenty of practice with encouraging smiles today. Especially with Ellie. Ellie had a Mogen David wine bottle, and you couldn't tell what she was supposed to be making out of it. She had whipped up a whole milk carton full of paste, most of which had already spilled on her desk top.

"Thicker paste, Ellie, and less of it," Mr. Forster said patiently.

Paul's bottle was the only one in the room that looked much like a person. His was a hunter. He'd made a little cap out of red felt and a rifle out of plastic tubing. Now Paul was painting the hunter's face.

"You'll probably get to be in the Fair," I said. I sighed, but not too loud. Sometimes it was a little sickening to have a best friend who was such a good artist.

Veronica Allison swept by my desk with her bottle person in her hand. She said, "Here, Mr. Forster. I'm finished."

"That's wonderful, Veronica. Who's your bottle supposed to be?"

"Greta Garbo," Veronica said.

"Oh. Of course, I should have known by the lonesome look in her eye."

Veronica looked pleased. She went back to her desk and started scrubbing it off. Veronica had her own pink sponge. It was the same color as her fingernails.

"Recess in ten minutes," Mr. Forster announced. "The rest of you should start thinking about cleaning up, too."

Just about everyone in the room jumped up and headed for the sink. Mr. Forster had to direct traffic to and from the circles. What with kids fighting over the class sponge and someone's bottle falling off a desk, it

92

took us almost twenty minutes to get the room back into shape.

At the end of all that time, Mr. Forster looked around, and there was Ellie Siegel, with paste dripping from the sides of her desk, still slapping paper and goo onto her wine bottle.

"Ellie," Mr. Forster said, and now his voice didn't sound so patient, "I want every bit of that cleaned up in five minutes flat. The rest of you are dismissed to the playground."

I didn't mind recess as much, now that we were playing kickball. For one thing, Paul was captain of my team. Paul had chosen me fifth, which was perfect, because it meant I got to stand in the middle of the line-up. I could get lost if I wanted to, or I could play, and I didn't have to be first or last, where people would notice me too much. Anyway, I was better at kickball than at softball. I still couldn't catch a ball, but at least I could kick one.

When Paul and I got to the bathroom, Mickey Blake was swinging from the top of a toilet stall and hooting at Robert Goldsmith, who was splashing water from the sink onto him.

"Okay, you guys," Paul said. "I don't want you getting the kickball wet again today. It's creepy to touch it afterwards."

Mickey pedaled like crazy in mid-air. "Not me. I'm a good little boy."

"I haven't even seen the ball," Robert said. He shadow boxed around Mickey's knees.

"Me either," Mickey said.

Paul groaned. "You're supposed to *have* the ball, Blake. It's your turn to take it out, all week. Remember?"

"Oh, yeah. Okay, chief. Right away, chief." Mickey dropped down. He clipped Robert's toe, and the two of them pretended to go into a headlock.

"I don't trust you, Blake. I'm coming up to the room with you," Paul said.

"Let's all go," Robert said from under Mickey's arm.

That's how the four of us happened to be in the empty classroom together during recess. Or at least, I thought it was empty—at first. Mickey went to the teacher's closet, where Mr. Forster kept the kickballs.

The teacher's closet was next to a row of six revolving doors that opened up into the coat closet. Each of the doors had a slate on the outside, so that when the doors were closed, they looked like a wall with a blackboard on it. The door on the end had a handle on the outside that opened or closed all of the doors at once. There used to be a handle on the inside, too, but it must have broken off a long time ago. Anyway, there wasn't one now.

The doors stood halfway open. Someone was rustling around among the coats, sweaters, and lunch pails inside.

"Hey, there's a mouse in here," Robert said.

Then I could see her. Ellie Siegel was fiddling around in the coat closet, with her coat half on and half off. The end of her scarf was in her mouth. She barely looked at us.

Mickey bounced the kickball off a blackboard. He pretended to ignore Ellie. "Hey, what's the matter with you guys? Aren't you good citizens? You know what Mr. Forster always says. Last one out of the coat closet closes the doors. Now here we are, all ready to go out to the playground, and those doors are wide open."

"So they are," Robert said loudly.

"Well? How about it?" Mickey said. "Are we going to do our duty, or aren't we?"

"Sure we are," Robert said, grinning.

Mickey grinned back. With one graceful kick, he turned the handle on the end door. The whole line of coat closet doors banged shut.

"Hey!" Ellie said from inside the closet. Something—probably Ellie's fist—thumped against one of the doors.

"Well, come on, guys. The whole game is waiting for this ball. Let's go," Mickey said.

I looked at Paul. Paul looked at me, then at Robert and Mickey. "Yeah," he said slowly. "We better get outside."

"But what about—" I stopped. The three of them were standing there, looking at me and waiting. Mickey's smile looked as if it might dive down into a frown any second.

By now Ellie was really banging on those doors.

Well, maybe it wouldn't hurt Ellie to spend her recess inside the coat closet. It would only be for twenty minutes or so.

"Okay," I whispered. "Let's go."

Mickey Blake slapped me on the back as we went out, so hard it hurt.

"Hey!" Ellie said again, but from the outside door, we could hardly hear her.

I was pretty nervous when Mr. Forster came back from the teachers' lounge after recess and lined us up to go back to class. I kept waiting for someone to notice that Ellie Siegel was missing. No one did. Ellie was always staying in at recess with "colds." Anyway, Ellie wasn't the kind of person who got worried about very much.

Paul and Robert were whispering to each other in front of me. They looked nervous, too. Not Mickey, though. There are some people who never smile, and there are other people who never look nervous or upset. It's as if their faces just won't fold into that shape. Mickey Blake looked like someone who was listening to jokes being cracked on an invisible radio.

As soon as we got to the classroom, we could hear the pounding on the coat closet doors. Ellie must have heard us coming. "Hey!" she called. I wondered if she'd been saying that same thing over and over for the last twenty minutes.

Mr. Forster looked puzzled. "What on earth—"

Then someone, I think it was Georgia Smith, realized. "Ellie Siegel never came out to recess. That's Ellie in there!"

96

Everyone laughed.

Mr. Forster headed for the closet doors at a fast clip. He yanked them open. Ellie stumbled out. Her coat was still halfway on, halfway off.

"I've always thought those doors were dangerous," Mr. Forster said tightly. "Are you all right, Ellie?"

Ellie didn't answer. Her face was white with rage. She looked straight at Mickey and Robert, and I was sure she was going to start screaming at them. Instead, Ellie stalked silently to her desk and sat down. She hadn't even taken off her coat. Tears started to dribble down Ellie's face.

Mr. Forster folded his arms. "Could someone explain to me exactly what is going on here?"

My mouth was so dry I didn't think I could open it.

Paul saved me the effort. He said, "We shut Ellie into the coat closet, Mr. Forster. You know, like for a practical joke." Paul wasn't looking at Mr. Forster.

"Who is 'we'?" Mr. Forster said.

So Robert, Mickey, and I told him.

Mr. Forster's lips got a white line around them. "I'll see you four out in the hall. The rest of you take off your things and begin page 104 in your arithmetic books." He opened the inside door for Paul, Robert, Mickey, and me.

Somehow the hall seemed darker than usual today. While Mr. Forster lectured us, I stared at the pools of shadow at our feet. Mr. Forster talked for a long time. About how Ellie might have suffocated in the coat closet, about how scared she must have been with no way to get out of there.

When he was done, even Mickey Blake looked guilty.

"Now then. I want the four of you to talk to your parents at noon. Tell them you'll be staying after school this afternoon, and tell them why. I'll see you again at 3:15." Mr. Forster went back into the room, leaving us out in the hall. Suddenly I felt stranded out there. All we had to do was follow Mr. Forster to our desks, but I didn't know if I could do it. I didn't want to see Ellie Siegel's face again.

When we did go back in, Ellie didn't look at any of us. She just stared straight ahead. By now, her coat was off.

That was a pretty bad moment. But talking to Aunt Zona at lunchtime was worse.

Aunt Zona went on and on. "If I were Mr. Foster, I'd take a paddle to you boys. I hope he does it. The very idea of shutting someone in a closet like that. When I was a girl, our next-door neighbor got locked in an ice box. She almost died." I could only hope she'd calm down by the time I got home that afternoon.

The hours dragged by until 3:15. I couldn't concentrate on anything. Not even English, my best subject.

When the dismissal bell rang, I automatically put my head down on my desk. The desk top was hard and cool. It smelled a little like paste. Please just bawl us out and then don't be mad anymore, Mr. Forster.

Mr. Forster didn't bawl us out. He didn't say anything at all. He just went to his desk, sat down, and

98

began grading papers. Paul, Robert, Mickey, and I sat there in absolute silence.

At least we had each other for company, even if we couldn't talk. It crossed my mind that this was the first time in my life I'd thought of someone like Mickey Blake as company. I wondered if Mickey had the same thoughts about me. Did this mean we liked each other now?

At 4:00, just when I thought I was going to scream from all that quiet, the outside door opened. A very fat woman with a pony tail walked in. "Oh, thank goodness you're here," the woman said. "I was about worried sick." After a minute I recognized her. She was Mickey Blake's mother. "I hope you know you've missed your appointment with the dentist, Mickey."

Mr. Forster stood up. "I'm sorry if you've been worried, Mrs. Blake. Didn't Mickey call you? He was supposed to."

"No one called me," Mrs. Blake said. "I'd like to know what my boy is doing up here at this hour, though."

"Why don't we discuss this outside?" Mr. Forster said. He led Mickey and Mrs. Blake out to the stoop. The door closed behind them, and that was the last I heard. When Mr. Forster came back in, Mickey and his mother weren't with him.

"All right, boys. I think you've learned your lesson. I'll see you tomorrow."

Paul, Robert, and I looked around at each other like

people who have just had a flashbulb go off in their faces. We got up stiffly.

"Good night, Mr. Forster," we muttered as we walked out.

"Good night," Mr. Forster said. His face had no expression at all.

By eight o'clock that night, things were back to normal at our house. Aunt Zona talked a lot more about ice boxes and suffocation during dinner, but gradually she got busy with other things and forgot about what had happened at school.

Right about eight, I was doing my arithmetic homework. Aunt Zona was cleaning the oven. While she was in the kitchen, the phone rang. "Get that, Billy Lou," she called. "I'm up to my elbows in Easy-Off."

I picked up the phone. "Hello?"

"Oh, is that Billy Lou? This is Mrs. Hardcastle, Billy Lou. How are you feeling tonight? I thought maybe your aunt would answer."

I said that I was fine and that Aunt Zona was cleaning the oven.

"Well, I just want to talk to her for a few minutes. About what went on at school today."

My stomach pitched. Mrs. Hardcastle sure had her ear to the ground to find out about that so fast. Now she was probably going to tell Aunt Zona how sinful I was to shut Ellie Siegel into the coat closet. That would send Aunt Zona off again. This time, she might even bring out the Bible.

But Mrs. Hardcastle didn't mention Ellie. She lowered her voice to a bare whisper and said, "By the way, Billy Lou, nothing really *happened* after school, did it? Before Mrs. Blake got there? Were any of you boys alone with Mr. Forster? You know you don't have to be afraid to talk about it. You can tell me anything."

For a minute I couldn't think of any way to answer. "I don't know if anything happened. I had my head on my desk most of the time. We were just sitting there, Mrs. Hardcastle."

Mrs. Hardcastle cleared her throat. "Of course you were. I knew that. It's just—well, you better run get your Aunt Zona for me. Tell her it's important."

So I got Aunt Zona. Aunt Zona grumbled a little as she peeled off her gloves. The whole kitchen stank, and there were dirty newspapers on the floor. "Of all times to be calling . . ." But she went to the phone.

I stood around in the dining room while Aunt Zona talked, so I could hear the worst. What I heard didn't make much sense, though. Once Aunt Zona said, "Yes, I guess that was pretty late to be keeping those boys." And another time, "I don't see what you mean, something 'funny' about him." Finally Aunt Zona said, "You know, little pitchers have big ears," which meant she didn't want me to listen to any more, and then she hung up.

For a long time after that, Aunt Zona stood by the phone. She looked at it the same way she looked at the TV when the vertical hold went out, as if she was just daring it to act up some more.

"What did Mrs. Hardcastle say, Aunt Zona?" I hopped from one foot to the other.

"She said . . . she didn't trust Mr. Foster. Didn't *trust* him." Aunt Zona chewed her lip. I waited for more. But Aunt Zona kind of shook herself and gave me a sharp look. "Say, Mr. Nosy, don't you have homework to do?"

"Well, yes, Aunt Zona, but . . ."

"No buts. Just get back to your books. I've got that oven to finish up. I can't stand here yakking all night. And quit your jiggling."

I sat down again at the dining room table, where my arithmetic book and my notebook were spread out. But I didn't go back to work right away. I sat there trying to puzzle out what was wrong with Mrs. Hardcastle. I guessed Mrs. Blake must have told her what happened at school. But Mrs. Hardcastle didn't sound mad at us kids. She sounded mad at Mr. Forster.

At last I picked up my pencil. Even thought problems were easier to figure out than Mrs. Hardcastle.

10

When something big happens, whether it's good or bad, it always seems to make you tired. You just want to rest for a long time afterward, and you don't want anything important to happen. That's the way it was for me for a few weeks after the day I got in trouble. I know that school went on as usual, but I don't remember much about what happened there. It was just school, and that's all.

Then, late in November, something big happened again.

It started on a cold, rainy afternoon before Thanksgiving. I had already finished the worksheet on indirect objects Mr. Forster had given us. Now I was staring out the gray streaky windows of Room 3. All the kids in the room were shifting around in their seats, like sleepers having bad dreams. Through the sounds of feet and paper shuffling, you could hear the monotonous *splat, splat* of the rain on the windows.

All at once, Mr. Forster said, "Pencils down, everyone." He had a big, red book in his hands.

Some of the kids looked up curiously. One by one, the pencils dropped.

"This rain is a vexation of the spirit," Mr. Forster said. "I think we all need something to combat it."

Claudia Hardcastle giggled softly. Veronica Allison was holding an index card up to her. It said:

YOUR NOSE IS RED.

Mr. Forster gave them a steady look. They got quiet.

"What's the book, Mr. Forster?" Paul asked.

Mr. Forster held it up. *"The Life and Adventures of King Arthur,"* he said. "I'm going to read you a few chapters. And while I read, I'd like you all to close your eyes and just forget about the rain. Forget about this room, this school. Forget about Kansas City. Instead, try to picture yourselves in England, over a thousand years ago. See if you can visualize the people and places I'm going to read about."

It's funny, but it really worked. Mr. Forster had a nice reading voice—smooth and even, but not boring like some teachers. When he got to the exciting parts, like Arthur pulling Excalibur out of the stone, he read faster, with lots of expression. And you could see it. The Sword flashed silver and made Arthur's skin look pale as he struggled to pull it out. Arthur began to break out in a cold sweat, but he didn't give up until the Sword began to move. And then it just slid out, as if under its own power.

The shuffling noises in Room 3 had stopped. Into the quiet, Mr. Forster said, "Now. Suppose we act out the scene I just read to you. Who'd like to be Arthur?"

Just about every boy in the room raised his hand—

104

and some of the girls, too. Mr. Forster picked Robert. Robert got up and pushed two chairs together in front of Mr. Forster's desk. He picked up the yardstick in the chalk tray and stuck it upright in the crack between the chairs. "This is the Sword in the Stone," Robert announced.

Then Robert backed to the inside door. From there he galloped up to the Stone on an invisible charger. When he pulled the Sword out, he panted and grumbled, as if the task were almost too much for him. In the end he held the Sword up high over his head. Robert looked a little like a prize fighter at the end of a bout. Everyone applauded, loud.

"Who's next?" Mr. Forster said.

Mr. Forster picked several other boys to play Arthur. Mickey Blake hammed it up and pretended to fall off his horse. The class laughed. Ricky Culligan made a thoughtful Arthur. He studied the Stone as if it were a crossword puzzle he was trying to solve. But no one else was quite as good as Robert had been.

After about fifteen minutes of this, Veronica Allison raised her hand. "This isn't fair, Mr. Forster," she said, jutting out her jaw.

"Why not, Veronica?"

"Arthur is a boy's part. What about a part for a woman?"

"There are lots of good parts for girls in the Arthur story," Mr. Forster said. "Morgan le Fay, Guinevere . . ."

"Well, I think we should act out the entire story. Especially the women's parts." Veronica crossed her arms. Most of the other girls nodded or said, "Yes."

Paul's hand shot up. "You know what, Mr. Forster? We ought to have a play about King Arthur. Tell about his whole life. With boys' parts, girls' parts, and everything. We could have scenery—"

"—and beautiful costumes for the actresses," Veronica put in.

"—and we could use the stage in the auditorium," Robert added. "With the lights and the curtains—"

"Hold on a minute." Mr. Forster laughed. "This is turning into quite an enterprise. A play is a lot of work, you know. How many of you think you'd be willing to put in the time?"

Every hand in the room went up. Some of the kids stomped their feet. "We want a play," Mickey chanted. A couple of boys joined in.

"All right, all right." Mr. Forster pretended to throw up his hands. "If the public demands a play, the play's the thing. Who am I to stand in the way?" But by the way he grinned, I could tell that Mr. Forster had been planning this all along. He didn't even look surprised. "The first thing we'll need, of course, is a script. I suggest that we elect a script committee. We'll give them a couple of weeks to read up on Arthur and write out the parts. I'll help the committee if they need it. And we'll need a chairman to supervise the writing. Do I hear any nominations for chairman?"

Heads turned to look at each other all over the room. No one said anything at first. Then Paul said, "Mr. Forster, I nominate Louis Lamb because he's the best writer in the room."

I felt myself blush.

"I second," Robert called out.

"Are there any other nominations?" Mr. Forster asked.

Claudia Hardcastle's hand inched up. Paul gave her a dirty look. Claudia's hand went back down.

"All in favor?"

The whole class said, "Aye."

I felt the blood rush to my head. A vein pounded in my throat. It was like being in a very fast elevator going up to the roof.

I was elected. *Me.*

Paul slugged me on the arm. He winked at me.

I winked, too, as well as I could with my eyelid twitching. And I slugged him back. Hard.

Counting me, there were three people on the script committee. The other two were Ricky Culligan and Georgia Smith. Georgia found most of the books about Arthur. Ricky threw in a couple of ideas, but mostly he messed around and daydreamed. I did the writing.

I never knew that writing could be so hard. When I wrote about the marvelous Mr. Mystifaction, ideas just popped into my head, and I never thought about the way one word followed another on the page. I was writing just for myself. But now, I had to write for the whole class. I had to think of words that each character could say, but they couldn't be just any words. They had to sound good on a stage, and they had to be interesting. Then, too, the play had to be long enough, but not too long.

Every few days Mr. Forster met with us and read what I'd written. We'd talk about it and make changes, then I'd go home and write it all over again. That was the worst part. Doing everything twice, or even three times. But Mr. Forster said that's the way real writers work.

When the script was finally done, I made a good copy in ink. Mr. Forster said he'd have it typed up and duplicated. At first I was going to write the good copy in the notebook Mr. Forster had given me. The one with the cover that looked like marble. I took it out of my drawer at home and even opened it to the first page. But something stopped me. This was supposed to be my "journal." I still wasn't sure what you wrote in a journal, but a play didn't seem like the right thing. So I put the notebook away and used regular paper instead.

A few days later, Mr. Forster gave a copy of the script to everyone.

"Those are my words," I thought. "My words."

All over the room, kids were sitting there reading what I had written. I watched their faces as they read. I watched to see who smiled, and when.

On page two, there was the scene where Merlin appears in Uther Pendragon's court in a puff of smoke, and Uther says, "By my troth, Merlin, you shouldn't always be popping in like that." Would anybody laugh at that line? I think Robert Goldsmith giggled a little. So did Ricky Culligan.

Then later on, the part where Morgan le Fay puts spider webs and bats' eyeballs into her cauldron to weave a spell—everyone ought to like that. But on the other hand, maybe the girls wouldn't want to play the scene. What would Veronica think, or Claudia?

When everyone finished reading, Robert Goldsmith looked up and said, "This is really good, Louis." *Louis.*

I got a funny feeling, kind of a cross between a tingle and a shiver. It felt good.

I don't think anyone called me Billy Lou for at least a day.

Then we had tryouts. Mr. Forster brought us all into the auditorium. Each kid got to go on stage and read some of the part he wanted to play. I read Merlin. It was scary to stand on that stage. With only thirty-five people in the room, the auditorium looked as big as the Cave of the Ozarks. I didn't like the way I had to yell my lines in order for everyone to hear me. It felt like something in the air was trying to snuff my voice out.

After me, Veronica Allison read Morgan le Fay. She was wearing her all-black outfit again. Veronica slinked all over the stage, and at the end she put in a hideous laugh that wasn't in the script. The laugh was the best part.

Tryouts lasted two days. They might have lasted even longer, since just about every boy in the room tried to read Arthur and every girl wanted to be either Morgan or Guinevere.

Mr. Forster announced the cast on a Friday afternoon. "I know you've all been waiting for the big news," Mr. Forster said. He took a list out of a notebook. "Well, here's the cast. Arthur: Robert Goldsmith." That was good. Robert had been the best at the audition. He even looked a little like my idea of

Arthur. "Guinevere: Claudia Hardcastle." Robert and Claudia made faces at each other. "Lancelot: Mickey Blake." Mickey gave a pleased smirk. Mickey wasn't my idea of Lancelot at all. "Merlin: Louis Lamb. Morgan le Fay: Veronica Allison." Mr. Forster kept reading, but I lost track of all the parts. Georgia, Ricky, and I had decided to make enough parts for everyone in the class to have at least one line. So it was a long, long list.

What I remember most is the understudies. "Understudies are very important," Mr. Forster told everyone. "Each major performer should work closely with his or her understudy, memorizing lines and so on. If for any reason a performer can't go on the day of the play, the understudy has to be prepared to do the part."

Everyone who didn't have a big part still looked sulky. Mr. Forster started reading the names of the understudies. Ricky Culligan was mine. Paul was Robert's. And Ellie Siegel was Veronica's.

When Mr. Forster read her name, Ellie began biting her thumb. Then she pulled her thumb out and stared straight at it. She watched it as if she expected something unusual to happen to it.

Veronica raised her hand. "Does everyone have to have an understudy?" she asked.

"Yes, Veronica. Everyone." Mr. Forster sounded firm.

"I'll bet Tuesday Weld never has an understudy," Veronica said.

Mr. Forster ignored her and kept reading names. Ellie's thumb went back in her mouth.

110

When he was done, Mr. Forster said, "I have some other news for you. I talked to Miss Cobb, and she has agreed to let us use the auditorium stage on Friday, December 19. That's the last day before Christmas vacation. We'll get to perform our play for the whole school. Parents, too, if they'd like to come."

We all clapped and cheered.

When the noise quieted down a little, Mr. Forster had us elect more committees. "Production committees," he called them. There was a scenery committee, a costume committee, a prop committee, a sound effects committee, a program committee, and an ushering committee.

I nominated Paul for chairman of the scenery committee. He won easily. Before the voting was even over, Paul had his colored pencils out and was sketching ideas on tablet paper.

At her desk, Veronica Allison made a sign on an index card. When Mr. Forster wasn't looking, she held it up.

UNFAIR TO ACTRESSES. ACTRESSES
SHOULD CHOOSE THEIR OWN UNDERSTUDIES.

I think Ellie Siegel must have seen the card out of the corner of her eye. She started in on her other thumb.

When the dismissal bell rang, Mr. Forster said, "Start learning your lines over the weekend, everyone. I'll see you Monday."

As we were putting on our jackets, Paul said, "This

111

whole play thing is going to be neat. Except for who's playing Morgan le Fay."

"You mean Veronica's understudy?"

"I mean Veronica. I can just hear her now. 'Hiya, Arthur. You'd be surprised.' "

"I know why Mr. Forster picked Veronica," I said. "It's because her natural clothes look just like a witch's. All black."

I picked up my books. Turning around, I almost knocked over a person behind me. Ellie Siegel, who was pulling on her navy blue coat.

"Sorry, Ellie," I muttered.

"Oh, sure you're sorry," Ellie said. For a minute I thought she was going to hit me. Ellie had a horrible expression on her face. You could almost call it hateful. But at the same time, Ellie looked pretty scared, even for Elllie.

Without saying anything more, Ellie pushed by me and ran for the door.

"What's eating her?" Paul said.

"I think she's upset about being Veronica's understudy."

"Oh, big deal," Paul said as we walked outside. "Wild horses couldn't keep Veronica from playing Morgan le Fay. Ellie doesn't have a thing to worry about."

"I guess not," I said.

Then Paul started telling me his ideas for the scenery. I forgot all about Ellie Siegel.

11

Thought for the Day
All the world's a stage.
> William Shakespeare.

I barely had time to copy down Claudia Hardcastle's Thought. I had too many other things to do today. Finish my arithmetic, then rush to the auditorium for rehearsal. At morning and afternoon recess, help Paul and the scenery committee paint a cardboard Camelot. During art class, make swords from cardboard and cover them with aluminum foil. Lucky thing that Georgia Smith's father ran an appliance store. Appliance stores always have plenty of cardboard cartons.

There were only two more weeks until the play. Two weeks, too, until Christmas vacation.

I didn't think I could stand it. "We should stop having arithmetic until after Christmas," I whispered to Paul. "There just isn't time for this stuff." I glared at my paper and tried to remember which fraction you invert when you divide two fractions. Dividing fractions didn't seem to follow any rule of nature at all. It was more like witchcraft than anything in King Arthur's time.

"How many towers do you think Camelot should have?" Paul asked.

"As many as we can paint on four refrigerator cartons."

"Felt!" Paul said.

"What?"

"Felt for the pennants! I forgot to bring it! I've got to call my mother. Mr. Forster, I've got to call my mother," Paul said, jumping up from his chair.

The whole morning was like that. Kids jumping up and down, running here and there to do this and that. Mr. Forster kept giving us seatwork to do, but he spent most of his time checking up on the different committees or rehearsing the actors.

During rehearsal I sat scrunched in a seat in the auditorium, a stack of books and papers on my lap, while Mr. Forster worked with Morgan le Fay and her flock of assistant enchantresses. Every now and then I copied down a spelling word or something, but most of the time I felt more like watching what was going on onstage. After all, those were my words the actors were saying, or supposed to be saying. Every time Veronica Allison or one of the other girls got her lines wrong, I winced. Sometimes Mr. Forster didn't even stop to correct them, and I felt like shouting the right words, but I never did.

Some of the kids had started wearing their costumes. Later on, we were going to have to use makeup.

Nothing fancy, Mr. Forster said, just a little rouge and eyebrow pencil to make our features stand out under the bright lights. I thought wearing makeup would be very strange, but of course it would be nothing new to someone like Veronica Allison.

Veronica had put on a black skirt with a slit up the side. When she walked, you could see that she was also wearing a ruffled black garter above her left knee. "How do you like my costume?" Veronica asked Mr. Forster. "It's not quite finished, of course."

Mr. Forster rubbed his chin. "Do you think the garter is absolutely necessary, Veronica? After all, you're supposed to be a medieval enchantress, not Gypsy Rose Lee."

Veronica and Mr. Forster argued about the costume for a while. While they were talking, Robert Goldsmith slipped out of his seat down the aisle and moved over next to mine. "Louis. Here," he whispered. Robert shoved an envelope at me.

"What's this?"

"It's an invitation to the cast party."

"What party?"

"Shhhh. Not so loud." Robert put his index finger on my lips. "Not everyone is supposed to know about it. It's going to be at my house, the night of the play, see. And there's going to be dancing."

I opened the invitation. It showed a boy with a flat-top haircut and a girl with a pony tail dancing together with their shoes off.

"I can't dance," I said.

"Oh, sure you can. Anyone can. And I can get you a date."

"A *date?*" I stared at Robert.

"Sure. It's going to be all couples. And everyone in the play is invited. Except." Robert pointed a few rows ahead.

"Except who?" I couldn't see who he was pointing to.

"Ellie Siegel." Robert barely mouthed the name. "That's why you're not supposed to talk about the party when she's around."

"Well, I don't—"

"See you." Robert bounced up and crept over to somebody else's seat.

I turned the invitation over and over in my hands. Part of me felt warm and happy. I'd never been invited to a party in this school. Not since I was in first grade, anyway. But I wasn't sure I wanted a date. Who in the world would it be? I couldn't imagine having any girl in our room for a *date.* I wasn't sure I wanted to dance, either. And Aunt Zona! What would she say about a party like this? With dates. I didn't even know what to tell her.

Then another thought came to me. Ellie. I didn't really think Robert should invite everyone in the play and then leave Ellie out. Sooner or later, Ellie was bound to find out about Robert's party, and I knew exactly how she was going to feel. What being left out does to your throat and your stomach, and how your eyes burn as you pretend you don't mind. Up until lately, I would have been left out, too. Of course, no one

116

in his right mind would want to be Ellie Siegel's date.

"Louis!" Mr. Forster's voice made me jump. "Get a move on. This is Merlin's scene coming up."

I raced to the stage.

While I was waiting in the wings for Merlin's cue, I turned to Paul, who was one of the knights. "Did you get invited to Robert's party?"

"Yeah."

"Do you think you'll go?"

"Sure. Why not?"

"But you have to have a *date*," I said, grabbing his arm. "Who are you going to get for a *date?*"

"Louis, let go of my arm. That hurts." Paul shook me off. "I don't really know. Someone."

"That was your cue, Louis," Mr. Forster called. "Wake up back there."

So then I had to pretend to appear onstage in a puff of smoke, and there was no time to think any more about the party.

At noon I thought about it again. I was sitting in the breakfast room at home, having a chunky-peanut-butter-and-grape-jelly sandwich with Aunt Zona. The breakfast room was really just a part of the kitchen with a table and chairs, a pink wicker basket full of ferns, and a chipped lamp shaped like a parrot that dangled on a slightly rusty chain from the ceiling.

I showed Aunt Zona the invitation Robert had given me. "Do you think I could go to this?" I asked softly. I shut my eyes for a second, half praying she'd say no, so

117

I wouldn't have to get a date—or worse, have Robert get one for me.

"If this isn't the cutest thing!" Aunt Zona said. "My goodness, Billy Lou, I just can't believe how fast you're growing up. Pretty soon now you'll be in high school. Your mother used to love to dance, you know. Of course, they didn't have rock and roll in those days."

"A lot of Baptists think that kind of dancing is a sin," I said quickly.

"Oh, I don't think there's any harm in it." Aunt Zona wiped a drop of milk off the soft, almost invisible hairs above her upper lip. "Not for someone your age."

I tried again. "Everyone at the party has to have a date, Aunt Zona."

"A date!" Aunt Zona crowed. "That's just precious. Who's going to be your date, Billy Lou?"

"I don't know," I said. I took an enormous bite of peanut butter and jelly and chewed it into a sticky glob so I wouldn't have to talk. I studied the chips in the parrot lamp over my head. Sometimes you just couldn't predict what a grown-up would say or do. They all seemed to have minds of their own.

Late that afternoon, I was in a corner of Room 3, standing on a bunch of newspapers, painting a tower onto a refrigerator carton. Paul and the rest of the scenery committee had mixed jars and jars of tempera, and there was so much painting to do that people pitched in whenever there was a spare minute.

"Hand me the blue, Louis," Frankie Burns said. I

passed it over. Just about everyone was beginning to call me Louis now. That was really the best thing about this play. Much better than being asked to Robert's party.

"Louis-s-s-s." Someone hissed in my ear. I turned. Veronica Allison was breathing on my neck.

"Oh, hi, Veronica." I went on painting.

"Louis, I've been thinking. Are you going to Robert's party?"

My brush slipped. A wavy gray line skittered down one side of the tower. "Who, me? Why?" If Veronica was going to ask me for a date, I was going to crawl inside this refrigerator carton, right here and now.

"Well, as I said, I've been thinking." Veronica flashed me a sugary smile. It didn't look right on her face. "You need a date for the party, and I need a date for the party."

Veronica was standing so close to my ear that she tickled it when she talked. I backed up a little, but that didn't stop Veronica.

"And you just happen to have a best friend who also needs a date for the party." Suddenly she was beginning to sound breathless, like Veronica-doing-Marilyn-Monroe again. "You know who I mean."

"Paul," I said.

"You know who," Veronica repeated. She licked her lips nervously. "Well. If you can get *him* to ask *me* to the party, *I* can get a date for *you*. My best friend, Claudia Hardcastle."

119

I made firm, hard strokes with my brush. "What if I don't want to go to the party with Claudia?"

Veronica stopped smiling. "You have to go with Claudia, Billy Lou. Who else do you think would go to a party with you? I mean, Claudia would be delighted to go with you. If I talk to her about it. Anyway, her parents won't let her go with anyone they don't know, and they know you from church, so—"

Maybe I *would* crawl into the refrigerator carton. No, Veronica would probably follow me in, still talking. "What do you want me to do, Veronica?"

"Just talk to you-know-who. Tell him I took dancing lessons last summer. Tell him I'd be a fabulous date. And I'll talk to Claudia. I'll tell her that you and she would make—a nice couple."

"Oh, all right, Veronica. But I don't know what Paul—"

Veronica pinched my arm.

"Ow. Hey, what's the matter with you?"

Veronica nodded at Ellie Siegel, who was headed our way with a script in her hand.

"You have to work on your lines with me. Mr. Forster said." Ellie gave Veronica a stubborn look, as if she was all geared up to have Veronica contradict her.

"I already know my lines," Veronica said coolly.

"We're supposed to work on them *together*. All the actors are supposed to work with their understudies."

"Okay." Veronica grabbed Ellie's script and flipped through the pages. "There. All done. Now I've worked on my lines with you." She tossed the script back at

Ellie, who dropped it. "I'm a speed reader," she said to me and anyone else who might happen to be listening. "We actresses call it a 'quick study.' "

Ellie bent over to pick up the script. When she straightened up, she looked like she was about to burst into tears. But she didn't. Ellie just walked over to her desk and sat down. She thumbed through her script, but her eyes seemed to be staring straight through it.

"Don't forget to talk to you-know-who," Veronica told me.

When the dismissal bell rang, I was still painting. Everyone else had cleaned up except Paul. He was cutting triangular pennants out of red felt. Pretty soon, we were the only ones left in the room except Mr. Forster.

"It's all beginning to look really splendid," Mr. Forster said.

"Thanks, Mr. Forster," Paul said. "We should be finished with all of the scenery by next week."

"That's good news. But right now, the two of you had better clean up and go home."

"Oh, Mr. Forster!" I moaned. "I just have a little bit more to paint on this tower. Can't we keep going a few more minutes?"

Mr. Forster ran his fingers through his thin hair. "I don't suppose you two busy artists have had a chance to look out the window in the past hour or so?"

"What do you mean?" Paul said. The two of us jumped up and took a look outside. The ground was covered with snow—at least an inch already, and the flakes were falling thick and fast.

"I'd say you'd better get going while the getting's good," Mr. Forster said. "You can finish this on Monday. Now come on. I'll help you pick these papers up."

There was no point in arguing. Mr. Forster's voice had a "that's final" tone to it. Paul and I started to put things away.

"Mr. Forster," I said, as I ran some brushes under the tap in the sink, "does it snow in Virginia?"

Mr. Forster laughed. "Of course, Louis."

"I always thought Virginia was warm, like Florida."

"Not as warm as Florida. Maybe the climate is a little milder than here. Where I lived, the weather wasn't much different from Kansas City's."

"Mr. Forster, will you go back to Virginia for Christmas?" Paul's voice was muffled. He was talking from behind a carton.

"I think so, Paul."

"That's where your family lives, isn't it?" I said. I screwed the lids on two paint jars.

Mr. Forster nodded.

"Is that where your writer friend is from, too? The one you told me about?"

Mr. Forster crumpled a thick wad of dirty newspapers and stuffed it into the wastebasket. "That's right. And now I think it's time for all of us to be off. This room looks good enough for the present." He walked back to the teacher's closet and began pulling on his coat.

Mr. Forster sure was in a hurry. Paul and I got our jackets and picked up our books.

We walked out with Mr. Forster. In front of the school his dirty blue Chevrolet stood coated with ice crystals and snowflakes. "Looks like your window needs scraping," Paul said.

"I'll help you, Mr. Forster!" I said.

"No, Louis. You'd better run along. Your aunt will be wondering what's become of you. Anyway, this won't take a minute."

"See you Monday," Paul said.

Paul and I started walking up the block. Snowflakes flew everywhere, into our noses and onto our eyelashes. The sidewalk was getting slick. "This looks like it's going to be a big snow," Paul said.

"I guess so." Something was bothering me. "Hey, do you think Mr. Forster's mad at us for some reason?"

"Why would he be mad at us?" Paul took a running slide that brought him to the corner of Fifty-ninth Street.

I took smaller skating steps. "I don't know. He just sounded like he didn't want us around."

"He didn't sound mad when he looked at our scenery."

"No." Cars were moving slowly along the snow-covered streets. A few had their lights on. Paul and I crossed Fifty-ninth Street and kept walking. When we were halfway down the next block, a horrible thought occurred to me. "Paul! You don't think somehow Mr. Forster found out that we made that phone call on Halloween?"

"How would he find out? We didn't even talk to him, remember? Anyway, that was a long time ago. Why would he suddenly get mad about it now?"

Paul was right. "I guess he just had someplace else to go today," I said.

"Like to the dentist. That would put anyone in a bad mood." Paul tilted back his head to catch a snowflake on his tongue.

By now we were almost at Fifty-fifth Street, where I had to turn off. I took a deep breath. Now might be a good time to mention something else. "About Robert's party. Um. Veronica Allison says she'd like to have you for a date. She, um, asked me to mention it. She says I can have Claudia for my date if you'll be hers. What do you think of that idea?"

Paul stopped for a minute. "What do I think of that idea? You want to know what I think of having Veronica Allison for a date?" Paul leaned over and picked up a gloveful of snow. He looked me in the eye. Then he grabbed me by the collar and stuffed the snow down my back.

"No fair! No fair!" I hopped around and reached inside my jacket and shirt to get the snow out. It was already melting. "You should be doing that to Veronica, not to me!" But I couldn't help laughing.

124

12

The week before Christmas vacation, Mr. Forster gave up altogether on trying to have class. Now everything was the play. Things kept happening that Mr. Forster called "Murphy's Law." Like: one day the custodian came across one of our cardboard boxes that hadn't been painted yet and took it out with the trash. Mr. Forster had to send an emergency committee over to Mr. Smith's appliance store to get another carton. Then Miss Cobb came to watch one of our rehearsals. She told Mr. Forster that Merlin couldn't appear in a cloud of smoke, fake or otherwise. She said I might get some kind of lung damage So we had to change that part of the script.

The worst thing happened two days before the show. Veronica Allison's grandmother died. Veronica had to go with her family to Sedalia for the funeral. She wouldn't be back until Friday night.

That meant Veronica's understudy had to play Morgan le Fay. Ellie Siegel.

Ellie was in tears when she found out. Mr. Forster had to take her out into the hall for a "private conference" to make her feel better.

"Look on the bright side," I told Paul. "At least you won't have to go to Robert's party with Veronica."

But now we had to have extra rehearsals with Ellie as Morgan. Veronica had left her slinky black costume at school, except for the garter. ("Maybe she plans to wear it to the funeral," I said to Paul.)

It was funny, though. With Ellie wearing it, Veronica's costume looked like nothing but a baggy house dress with a slit up the side.

"Couldn't your mother take that costume in a little for you?" Mr. Forster asked Ellie.

"My mother doesn't sew," Ellie mumbled.

At least Ellie knew her lines. She wasn't very loud, but she didn't forget anything. Ellie didn't exactly look happy, but then, Morgan was a witch, and witches don't have to look happy.

"You're doing just fine, Ellie," Mr. Forster kept saying. He made the class applaud for her. It wasn't very loud applause, but it was applause. Ellie looked a little less miserable.

While all this was going on at school, Paul and I were working on a secret project. Our Christmas present to Mr. Forster. Actually, it was my present. It was my idea. Paul was just helping.

I really wanted to buy Mr. Forster something. After all, Mr. Forster had just about changed my whole life. Even my name. He made the kids call me Louis. Well, he didn't exactly *make* them do it, but they did it. It was just like I'd planned it back in September. No more Billy Lou. Mr. Forster had to be the best teacher in

Kansas City if he could make that happen. Maybe the best teacher in the world.

But I couldn't afford to buy him anything. Aunt Zona had given me a dinky little Christmas allowance. Just enough to buy her what she said she wanted for Christmas: a package of hose from J. C. Penney's basement.

So I decided to make something. A giant Christmas card, three feet tall, with a cover picture by Paul and a poem by me. Paul and I had borrowed some extra cardboard from Mr. Smith's store. I had carried it home to Aunt Zona's, and we were finishing the card in the afternoons.

Paul was painting a Santa Claus on the front. Santa looked a little bit like Mr. Forster—just enough for Mr. Forster to get the point. The poem was hard to write. I started it on notebook paper, then tore it up, then started it again. The version I ended up writing on the inside of the card went like this:

> To a superlative teacher, you're the best,
> We like you better than all the rest.
> Your helpful ways have taught us most,
> So here's a Merry Christmas toast
> and Happy New Year
> from
> your friends
> Louis Lamb and
> Paul Harte

I told Paul to add a champagne glass in Santa's hand for the toast part, but Aunt Zona heard me. She said that wine is a mocker and strong drink is raging and we couldn't put something like that on a Christmas card. So we didn't.

The day of the play Paul and I sneaked the card into the coat closet while Mr. Forster wasn't looking. That wasn't hard. Mr. Forster kept dashing back and forth from the auditorium. He didn't pay much attention to what was going on in the room. Mickey Blake stood up on top of a desk pretending to fight a dragon and Mr. Forster didn't even notice. Just to be on the safe side, Paul and I draped our coats over the Christmas card to hide it. We were going to surprise Mr. Forster after the performance.

Every other class in the school had been asked to come, and Mr. Forster had made us write personal invitations to our families as part of English class. The play was gong to be at two o'clock. That morning, Mr. Forster had us do one last run-through with Ellie Siegel as Morgan.

Ellie's face had a pasty look, but she had her part down pat. She even tried to laugh like a witch. The laugh came out as a kind of squawk. Ellie kept wiping her palms on her baggy costume.

Ellie wasn't the only nervous one. After we finished the rehearsal, the auditorium suddenly looked very spooky. For no reason at all, everyone started to whisper instead of talk. Mr. Forster gave the class a little speech. "I can't tell you how proud I am of each and every one of you," he said. "I know your play is going to be a huge success. And the best part is, you did it all yourselves."

I didn't go home for lunch that day. Robert, Paul, and I sat on the stage and ate sandwiches, wearing our makeup and costumes. I tried to picture the auditorium as it would be in just an hour and a half, the seats full of people watching me play Merlin, listening to all the lines I had written. Aunt Zona would be in the front row. So would Mrs. Harte and Mrs. Goldsmith.

Ellie Siegel was sitting in an auditorium seat by herself, a few rows back and off to one side. She twirled her straw around in her milk carton. When she sipped, Ellie made loud slurping noises. I wondered if Ellie had found out yet about Robert's cast party. Suddenly it seemed that I ought to say something to Ellie, anything to make her feel like she belonged in the play. So I called out, "Hey, Ellie. Good luck this afternoon."

"You're supposed to say, 'Break a leg,' " Robert told me.

"Okay. Break a leg, Ellie."

Ellie looked up. She had a startled look on her face. I wondered if she understood what I meant. Then Ellie opened her mouth and out came a loud hiccup. And another. And a minute later, another.

Paul and Robert started to laugh. But Ellie kept hiccuping. "This isn't funny," I said. "She can't stop."

Georgia Smith walked into the auditorium with an armload of cardboard swords. When she noticed Ellie, she ran over to Ellie's chair and started slapping her on the back.

"Hic. Stop it! Hic," Ellie gasped, and pushed Georgia

away. Patting her own chest, Ellie darted out the back door.

"I think Mr. Forster would call this 'Murphy's Law,'" Robert said. "Personally, I think it's psychosomatic."

"Somebody ought to tell Mr. Forster," I said.

Georgia headed back to the classroom to find him.

Ellie spent the next half hour in the girl's restroom. Mr. Forster kept sending Georgia in to check up on her. "She's not puking, she just has the hiccups," Georgia told everyone.

"I'm sure Ellie will be fine when the play starts," Mr. Forster said.

She wasn't.

For the hour before the play, Mr. Forster had Ellie sit back at her desk, taking deep breaths and thinking relaxing thoughts. He told her to think about the Alps and all that quiet beauty. Ellie said she'd never been to the Alps. She kept hiccuping.

About ten minutes before show time, Mr. Forster took us to the auditorium. We got to enter by the stage door. Everyone scrambled around on tiptoe, trying not to let the audience know we were there. People had started gathering already—mostly the mothers, so far. I could hear them talking and laughing out front. Even though I was supposed to be waiting in the wings, I couldn't resist taking a peek through the curtain. Aunt Zona and Mrs. Harte walked in together. At the back door, Miss Rosenthal appeared with her kinder-gartners. Miss Rosenthal kept her index finger pressed

130

tightly against her lips as she led them down the aisle. Then Mr. Forster waved me away, so I didn't get to see any more.

I put my hand against my stomach, where a whole tribe of butterflies seemed to be flapping around. It wasn't just that I was nervous about doing my own part well. I was worried about the way everyone else was going to say the lines I wrote. It was like having stage fright for thirty-five people at once.

When the curtain went up, Ellie Siegel was standing in the wings, bending over and trying to put her head between her legs because someone told her that might help her hiccups. Ricky Culligan, who was the narrator, walked out on the stage. He started his speech. We could hear Ellie hiccup all the way through it. I wondered if the audience could hear her as well as we could. There was no way of telling. The bright lights hid their faces from anyone on the stage.

"Thought for the Day," Robert said loudly. "The show must go on."

Mr. Forster gave him a disapproving look.

I don't know why it is that when something great that you plan for actually comes off, it always goes by so fast. Even while I was on stage, saying the lines I'd written to a roomful of people, it seemed like one of those speeded-up films on TV. When it was over, I couldn't believe that any of it had happened. Only I was soaked with cold sweat.

I don't know how it felt to Ellie. Maybe it all seemed like slow motion to her. At any rate, Ellie never

131

stopped hiccuping. She hiccuped all the way through three acts. The audience was very polite. When Ellie was on, nobody coughed. Not even the kindergartners in the second and third rows. Somehow I think that made Ellie feel worse. Every time she came offstage, she looked paler.

After the final curtain came down, Ellie sat on a stool by the light switches and refused to budge. She wouldn't take her bows. The audience really seemed to like the play. They applauded for a long time, and we got to take three curtain calls. But that didn't matter to Ellie.

"Louis, you were terrific," Robert said, slapping me on the back. "Way to go, babe."

I didn't answer him. I was trying to hear what Mr. Forster was saying to Ellie. He had an arm around her shoulders, and he looked very sympathetic, but Ellie wouldn't even glance at him.

Finally Mr. Forster gave up on Ellie. A lot of the mothers were coming backstage, and Mr. Forster had to talk to them.

It was only then, when people started saying how good the play was and how interesting, that I really began to feel proud. After all, I was the author.

Aunt Zona came back with Mrs. Harte and gave me one of her hardest squeezes. Merlin's tall pointed hat fell off my head. "You were just fine, Billy Lou. You were born for the stage, just like your mother." While she had me in her grip, Aunt Zona whispered, "Don't you worry about that little girl with the hiccups. She didn't spoil a thing. When she talked, I just repeated all the words, so people could understand them."

"Congratulations, fellows," Mrs. Harte said, beaming. "You were great. Love that scenery—and that script, too."

Sometime during all of the congratulating, Ellie Siegel disappeared. I don't think anyone missed her but me.

Mrs. Harte had to pick Paul's sister up at her special school right away, so Paul couldn't stick around to give Mr. Forster the Christmas card. I had to do it myself, which was okay with me. I wanted Mr. Forster to know that the card had been my idea.

Aunt Zona waited in front of the school while I went back to Room 3. Mr. Forster came in just as I was dragging the card out of the closet.

The room was dark with late afternoon shadows. Mr. Forster didn't believe in wasting electricity while the class was in the auditorium. By now almost everyone had gone home, so he didn't bother to turn the overhead lights back on.

"What's all this?" Mr. Forster said.

"This is your Christmas present, Mr. Forster. It's from me. Paul helped."

Mr. Forster pulled the card close to the windows, where the light would hit it. He looked at the Santa Claus for a long time with a kind of half-smile on his face. "You shouldn't have gone to so much trouble," he said softly.

133

"Read the inside, Mr. Forster. That's the part I wrote."

Mr. Forster opened the card wide. As he read my poem, his face went almost blank.

"Do you like it?" I said after a minute.

Mr. Forster looked at me over the top of the card. When he spoke, he sounded hoarse. "Louis, it's unique. I think it's the best Christmas present I've had in a long, long time." Mr. Forster walked around the Christmas card. He touched my shoulder lightly. "Thank you."

"Oh, there you are, Mr. Forster." Mrs. Hardcastle's voice came from the inside doorway. "I just stopped in to congratulate you on the wonderful play. My, it's dark in here. Is that you, Billy Lou? Your Aunt Zona is standing outside in the cold waiting for you."

I turned around. "Oh. Okay, I'm coming. Merry Christmas, Mr. Forster."

"Merry Christmas, Louis."

Mrs. Hardcastle put her hand on my elbow and walked out with me. When we left the room, Mr. Forster's lips were moving silently. He was reading the card again.

13

I blew into Paul's face. We were in the back seat of his father's car on our way to the cast party. "What do you think? Is my breath okay?"

Paul held his nose. "It's like fried salami."

I jammed my hand into my sport coat pocket, trying to find the peppermint Life Savers Aunt Zona had put in there before I left home.

Paul stopped me. "Relax. I was just kidding. You smell fine."

Mr. Harte turned a corner onto Forest Street. He began to slow down. "I think it's the next block, Gerald," Mrs. Harte told him. Mr. Harte speeded up again.

Thank goodness Claudia was going to meet me at Robert's house. At least I wouldn't have to pick her up at the Hardcastles' and try to think of things to say to Reverend and Mrs. Hardcastle. For that matter, as long as Claudia and I would only be together at the party, I wouldn't have to think of things to say to Claudia, either. We might not have to talk at all.

"You lucked out," I said to Paul. "I wish I got to be stag, too."

"I hope Veronica stays in Sedalia for the rest of her life," Paul said.

"This is it, Gerald." Mrs. Harte pointed to a big brick house with all the lights on. Mr. Harte pulled into the driveway. "We'll be back at the stroke of midnight," Mrs. Harte said. "Be sure you're ready, you two."

I was ready to go home now, but I didn't say so. I still didn't know what in the world I would do if Claudia wanted to dance with me. We got out of the car and walked up the Goldsmiths' porch steps. Paul put his hand out to ring the bell, but the door opened before he even pushed it.

Veronica Allison stood in the doorway. "Surprise! We got back from the funeral just before dinner. I wasn't about to miss our first big date," she said to Paul.

Paul's face turned a funny color. It could have been the yellow porch light that made him look that way. "Hi, Veronica," was all he said.

Veronica let us in. She was wearing her peasant blouse and a black skirt, not as slinky as the one she had made for Morgan le Fay. As Paul and I walked into the Goldsmiths' living room, Veronica hitched one side of her skirt up. She was wearing Morgan le Fay's ruffled black garter. "You like?" she said.

"It's real nice, Veronica," Paul said. Both of us looked around, but we were the only ones in the room. Music was thrumming somewhere else in the house.

"The party's downstairs, in the rec room. Follow me. You too, Bil—Louis." Veronica led us to a door in the

136

kitchen. We all went down a flight of steps into a big room with wood paneling.

Robert's record player was turned up almost all the way. Two people were dancing in the middle of the rec room. Robert and his mother. A bunch of kids were standing by the refreshment table, munching potato chips and watching.

Annette Funicello was singing "Tall Paul."

Every time Annette sang the words "he's my all," Veronica gave Paul a kind of under-the-eyelashes look and showed her garter. Paul said, "Let's get some potato chips." He had to yell it in my ear, but I heard him. Veronica followed us to the refreshment table.

Claudia Hardcastle was standing by the onion dip.

"Hi," I said.

"Hi," Claudia said.

We looked at each other.

"Is that good dip?" I said.

"Yah," Claudia said.

We looked at each other some more.

Annette Funicello finished up and another record dropped down. A slow one. "Sixteen Candles."

"Come on, everybody," Robert shouted over the opening bars. "You're not dancing."

Robert's mother smoothed her skirt. "I think I'd better get back upstairs and greet the other guests," she said. "You kids have fun." Mrs. Goldsmith left the room.

Robert walked over to us. "Maybe I should put on another fast one," he said after a minute.

"Maybe so," I said.

More kids were coming down. Now just about the whole sixth grade was there. Except Ellie Siegel, of course. I wondered what Ellie was doing tonight. And if she was over her hiccups yet.

Robert put on "Rock and Roll Is Here to Stay." Mickey Blake started to dance with Georgia Smith. A few other couples began to dance, too. I looked at Claudia out of the corner of my eye. Claudia was looking at me out of the corner of her eye.

I tugged at my shirt collar. It felt like Aunt Zona had used a whole bucket of starch on it. I counted the people dancing. Twelve. "Uh," I said. "Maybe we should dance, Claudia."

Claudia shrugged.

Paul and Veronica were out on the floor now. Veronica was leading. Paul was a pretty good dancer, but of course Veronica was bigger than he was. Every now and then Veronica lifted Paul's arm and ducked to turn herself.

I touched Claudia's hand. Her palm was clammy, but then so was mine. "Well, let's dance," I said.

After a while, it wasn't so bad. Robert kept playing fast records, which made me out of breath, but I didn't have to get too close to Claudia. Claudia stepped on my toes now and then. Not too hard, though. I didn't try to turn her.

By the time Annette Funicello came on again, I was ready to rest. I was sweating, and I wanted to take my tie off, so I gently pushed Claudia back to the onion dip. The other couples were giving up, too. Paul walked up to me with a handful of potato chips.

Claudia went over to where Veronica was standing, and the two of them started whispering to each other and giggling. Then Veronica said grandly, "If you gentlemen will excuse us, we'll visit the powder room now." They swept by us on their way to the stairs.

Robert was nearby, listening. "Too much excitement can affect the kidneys," he said in the voice he used for diagnosing people. "With some persons, it gets to be a chronic condition."

Claudia and Veronica didn't come back for a long time. Paul, Robert, and I watched Mickey Blake dance by himself. Mickey was good. He could do a half-splits and get back up again without getting very far behind the music.

After a while Mrs. Goldsmith marched back down into the rec room. Veronica and Claudia were at her heels. Both of them had put on a thick coat of lipstick, and they reeked of perfume. "Now I don't want to hear another word about it," Mrs. Goldsmith was telling Veronica. "The party's down here, and you girls belong with the other children, not prowling around upstairs." She dropped Veronica and Claudia off by the punch bowl and left the room.

Robert sniffed. "That smells like my mother's perfume," he said accusingly.

Veronica ignored him. "How about another dance, big boy?" she said to Paul.

Paul hemmed and hawed. "I'm a little tired, Veronica . . ."

"Well, if you don't want to!" Veronica suddenly sounded cross. She and Claudia put their heads to-

139

gether, then folded their arms and stood there, looking sulky.

Now the party moved very slowly. Nobody danced. Nobody talked much, either.

Just when I was starting to feel really bored, Mrs. Goldsmith appeared at the top of the stairs carrying an enormous chocolate cake. "Look who's here, everyone," she said.

Mr. Forster walked down the steps behind her.

I cheered. So did some of the other kids.

"I thought that since this party is in honor of the class play, Mr. Forster ought to be here, too. So I called him, and he was nice enough to drop by for a few minutes. And look what he brought!" Mrs. Goldsmith set the cake down on the refreshment table.

"I think there ought to be enough for everyone to have a small piece," Mr. Forster said. He took a knife and began slicing up the cake. Everyone got a piece on a party napkin. Mrs. Goldsmith went back upstairs for more napkins.

With Mr. Forster there, the party picked up. When Robert played "Blue Suede Shoes," Mr. Forster clicked his fingers and sang along. Everybody laughed. Then kids began to dance again.

I almost decided to ask Claudia one more time, but she and Veronica were in a huddle again. Pretty soon they went out on the floor and started dancing with each other.

"Looks like they've given up on us," Paul said, sounding relieved.

"Well, so much for your first big date with Veronica Allison," I said. Paul hit me, but he grinned.

Because we weren't dancing, Paul and I were the first to see what happened then. It started with a commotion at the top of the steps: voices loud enough to be heard over the music. The door to the kitchen banged open. Paul and I looked up.

Ellie Siegel's mother came down the stairs with hard, quick steps, pulling Ellie along behind her. Mrs. Goldsmith was behind Ellie, trying to keep up with the two of them.

I don't know why, but I didn't really hear what they were saying at first. I kept staring at Mrs. Siegel's shoes. They were bright red, with pointy toes, and polished to a shine, so that the lights of the rec room were reflected up in them.

The first thing I actually heard Mrs. Siegel say was, "I might have known *you'd* be here. Oh, yes." Then I had to look up. Mr. Forster was standing across the room by the record player, but it was clear that Mrs. Siegel was talking to him.

"Well, isn't this a lovely party," Mrs. Siegel said. By now everyone had stopped dancing. Mr. Forster lifted the needle off the record that was playing. It came up with a scratching sound. "I certainly don't want to spoil your good time, Mr. Forster. I just want to know why my daughter was not invited to this class party."

Ellie looked as if someone had punched her in the stomach. She didn't look at her mother. She didn't look at anyone.

141

"Mrs. Siegel. Ellie—I—oh, I'm so sorry. Believe me, I didn't realize." Mr. Forster took a step forward, then stopped. He glanced over at Mrs. Goldsmith.

Mrs. Goldsmith had a wild look on her face. "Robert—" she said, her arms moving helplessly. Robert ducked away, blushing.

I wanted to be somewhere else. Anywhere else. And right now. But I couldn't move. Nobody could.

"This is your fault," Mrs. Siegel shouted. "I hold you personally responsible, Mr. Forster. You humiliated this child at school by forcing her to perform in a part she wasn't prepared for. And if that wasn't enough, this."

Mr. Forster said, "Oh, Ellie." He took another step.

"I don't know what you have against my daughter, Mr. Forster, but you've obviously been persecuting her all year. And I want you to know, it's going to stop." Mrs. Siegel took a quick breath. "You think you can get away with anything, don't you. I know all about you. Everybody knows what you are, but nobody's had the guts to do anything about it. Well, *I'm* going to do something about it. You're no kind of teacher, Mr. Forster. You don't deserve to be in a public school. And you mark my words, you won't be much longer."

Mrs. Siegel took another breath. She looked around the room as if she'd forgotten how she came in. Then she turned and pulled Ellie back up the steps. She didn't look back, and neither did Ellie.

And still, no one moved.

Mrs. Goldsmith said, "Oh, my God."

14

It's strange, but I don't remember coming home from Robert's party. I just know that all during Christmas vacation, I tried to forget about it. Most of the time, there were plenty of other things to think about. After I bought Aunt Zona's present, I had to worry about getting enough paper and ribbon to wrap a package of hose. Aunt Zona must have thought about this herself, because one day I found a square of green wrapping paper and some ribbon already tied in a big bow on my bed. On Christmas morning I had to think about keeping a happy expression on my face while I unwrapped the underwear and pajamas Aunt Zona always gave me. This year she gave me a game called Clue and two Hardy Boys books, too.

Still, I couldn't shake the feeling that something terrible was going to happen when vacation was over. "Everybody knows what you are," Mrs. Siegel had said. I wasn't at all sure what she was talking about, but I believed that she hated Mr. Forster. And I believed her when she said she was going to "do something about it."

One morning just before New Year's, I was in my

bedroom reading when the telephone rang. I went to answer it. It was Mrs. Hardcastle asking to talk to Aunt Zona. Mrs. Hardcastle didn't say much to me, but I knew bad things were happening. I knew it by the way Aunt Zona said, "Billy Lou, you know it isn't polite to listen in on your elders when they're talking on the phone," and sent me back to my room.

I tried to listen from my bedroom door, but I couldn't catch what Aunt Zona was saying to Mrs. Hardcastle. That scared me. Aunt Zona always talked loud.

I got my china animals together and spread them out on the floor around me. I sat in the middle of the magic circle and stared at the unicorn. I tried to make the animals dance. I looked at the animals through my eyelashes. I closed my eyes and waited. But I kept hearing whispers from the dining room where Aunt Zona was talking to Mrs. Hardcastle. The animals didn't dance. They looked tiny and stiff. I just sat there for a long time, even after Aunt Zona got off the phone.

I don't know what I expected to happen the day after vacation, but when I walked into Room 3 that morning I kept looking around the room, as if something might jump out from behind a desk. Nothing did. Mr. Forster was standing very calmly at the blackboard, writing:

January 5, 1959. Happy New Year!

His *p*'s still had the extra loops on them. Ricky Culligan was standing by another square of blackboard, writing the Thought for the Day. Everything was the same as usual.

144

Ellie Siegel was absent, but that wasn't unusual. Ellie got sick all the time.

In arithmetic, we were still on fractions. Mr. Forster showed us again how to invert when you divide two fractions. That was normal, too. I began to relax a little.

Around ten o'clock the inside door opened. Mrs. Hardcastle, Mrs. Blake, and Mrs. Siegel walked in. And then I knew that things were not going to be normal, after all.

Mrs. Hardcastle did all the talking. She was wearing the same smile she used on our Young Galileans class on Sunday mornings. "Good morning, Mr. Forster. You go right ahead with your lesson, and don't pay a bit of attention to us. We're just here to observe."

Mr. Forster didn't smile back. "I'm always glad to see parents at school," he said. "But classroom visitors usually have to get permission from the principal."

"Oh, we have permission. We've already had a talk with Miss Cobb," Mrs. Hardcastle said.

"I see." Mr. Forster turned to the blackboard and began to write a fractions problem. He said, "Just sit wherever you like." Mr. Forster went on with arithmetic. He didn't say anything to the three mothers. But every time he wrote something on the board, he pressed down too hard on the chalk. He left little white spots that wouldn't erase.

I tried not to look at Mrs. Hardcastle, Mrs. Blake, and Mrs. Siegel. But after they came, I couldn't concentrate on fractions. It wasn't that Mr. Forster didn't explain them well. I just couldn't keep my mind on arithmetic.

When it was recess time, the parents stood up.

"If you don't mind, Mr. Forster, we'd like to go out to the playground with the children. Just to observe a little more," Mrs. Hardcastle said.

"Certainly. We'd be glad to have you." Mr. Forster didn't look glad as he got his coat out of the closet.

We lined up. Mrs. Hardcastle and Mrs. Siegel got in the girls' line. Mrs. Blake got at the head of the boys' line.

"The class is going to stop off at the restrooms. Maybe you'd like to meet us on the playground," Mr. Forster said.

"Oh, I don't think so," Mrs. Hardcastle said. "We want to see the whole routine. We'll just go down to the restrooms with the children. In fact, that'll give you time for a cup of coffee if you'd like one, Mr. Forster."

Mr. Forster turned scarlet. He started to say something, then stopped.

"You can't go into the boys' bathroom, Mother," Mickey Blake hissed.

Mrs. Blake whispered something in his ear. Mickey shut up.

As it turned out, Mrs. Blake and Mr. Forster both stood outside the bathroom door while the boys went in. It made me feel nervous to have the two of them out there, just staring at each other. I couldn't do anything in the bathroom except wash my hands.

The mothers stayed right with us for the rest of the

morning. When the noon bell rang, they got up quietly and left. I felt as if I'd been holding one breath all morning. Finally I could let the air out.

But that wasn't the end of the visit. After lunch, the same three mothers were back, only now Mrs. Allison, Mrs. Harte, and Mrs. Goldsmith were with them. Mr. Forster met the parents at the door. He said something in a very low voice.

Mrs. Siegel said loudly, "Yes, I'm sure it's not convenient for you to have us here this afternoon, or any other afternoon. But you just get it through your head, Mr. Forster. We're going to keep right on coming back."

Mrs. Goldsmith tugged at Mrs. Siegel's coat sleeve. Mrs. Siegel shook her off.

Mrs. Harte said, "It's nothing personal, Mr. Forster. Please believe that. But we have our children's interests to protect."

"What seems to be the problem here, Mr. Forster?" Miss Cobb made her way through the clot of parents at the door. She sounded just like she did when she patrolled the tables in the cafeteria, trying to keep kids from talking while they ate.

The whole bunch of them went out into the hall and closed the door behind them. Usually when the teacher leaves the room, kids start clowning and acting up. This time, nobody did anything but whisper.

"I can't stand it," I told Paul. "What do you think's going on out there?"

Paul just shrugged, but Veronica Allison gave

147

Claudia Hardcastle a knowing look. Claudia smirked back.

After ten minutes had gone by, Veronica stood up. "I'm going to peek," she announced.

Robert Goldsmith said, "You can't go out there, Veronica. Cobb will eat you alive and spit out the pieces."

"No, she won't. I'll tell her I have to go to the bathroom. And I'll walk real slow, so I can see what's going on. You just wait." Veronica was out the door before anyone could say anything else.

While she was gone, the only sound in the room was the hum of the electric clock on the wall. I found myself wondering why some clocks hum and some don't. Then I decided that was a pretty stupid thing to be wondering about.

Veronica seemed to take forever to come back. When she finally showed up, she told us, "They're in the office, just sitting around. Mrs. Goldsmith is arguing with Mrs. Siegel. I couldn't hear much."

The inside door opened behind Veronica. "What are you doing out of your seat?" Mr. Forster yelled. I'd never heard him talk that way to anyone. Before Veronica could say anything, Mr. Forster cleared his throat. Then he said softly, "I'm sorry, Veronica. Sit down, please."

The mothers didn't come back that day. But that night, and for three nights afterward, Aunt Zona kept getting phone calls. Every time the phone rang, Aunt Zona answered it herself. She always sent me out of the room, even if I was doing homework on the dining

148

room table. She never told me what the calls were about.

At school, Ellie Siegel's desk stayed empty all week.

On Friday afternoon, we were having social studies when Miss Cobb came to the door. "I wonder if I could see you in my office for a few minutes, Mr. Forster."

Mr. Forster took his pointer off the wall map of Europe.

Miss Edmonds, the music teacher, appeared in the doorway. "I'll just keep an eye on these people while you're gone, Mr. Forster."

Mr. Forster nodded and followed Miss Cobb into the hall.

While he was gone, Miss Edmonds sat on Mr. Forster's desk, swinging her legs. I noticed that she had varicose veins under her brown stockings. She didn't try to teach us anything.

Mr. Forster was gone much longer than a few minutes. I took out my library book, but I couldn't read. Paul and I tossed a note back and forth. We drew cartoons of monsters and superheroes on it. Paul's were better than mine. After a while, I couldn't bring myself to draw, either.

Mr. Forster came back just before time to go home. His face was white. When he got to his desk, Mr. Forster put his fingers out as if to balance himself against the edge. Miss Edmonds left.

The dismissal bell rang. Mr. Forster didn't seem to hear it. After a few minutes, everyone began to put books and papers away. I tried to get in and out of my

149

desk without making any noise at all. I think the other kids did, too. We kept waiting for Mr. Forster to say something. When he finally spoke, it was almost in a whisper. "All right. Class dismissed."

Claudia Hardcastle let out a nervous giggle. Then everybody got up slowly. Mr. Forster walked to the teacher's closet and pulled out his coat. He left the room without even putting it on.

Paul and I looked at each other. I couldn't think of anything to say. I felt a big knot growing in my stomach.

The knot stayed in my stomach all weekend. I didn't know how to make it go away. I didn't mention it to Aunt Zona, though. She would have just made me take Milk of Magnesia.

On Monday morning when I walked into Room 3, Mr. Forster wasn't there. Miss Cobb was standing by Mr. Forster's desk. A tall thin woman stood next to her. The woman had gray hair pulled back into a bun, only some of the hairs escaped over her ears. While all the kids hung up their coats, the woman kept her hands folded tightly in front of her. Everyone seemed to be whispering to everyone else.

As soon as the bell rang, Miss Cobb started talking. "Boys and girls, I have sad news for you. Mr. Forster has been called away suddenly, so he won't be able to be with us at Alcott School for the rest of the year. This is Mrs. O'Dowd. She'll be your substitute teacher until we can find a replacement for Mr. Forster. I know you'll show her every courtesy."

"That's not fair!" The words came out of my mouth before I could stop them. Miss Cobb turned to give me one of her coldest stares. Everyone else deliberately kept from looking at me. Almost automatically, I waved my hand.

"What is it, Billy Lou?"

"I don't understand. What happened to Mr. Forster? He wouldn't just leave without telling us. Mr. Forster isn't like that." As I talked, I felt tears begin to sting my eyes. My tongue got that heavy feeling in back, and I couldn't swallow.

"As I said, Mr. Forster was called away suddenly. I'm sure he'll miss you all very much. Now then, let's get to work." Miss Cobb stood there until everyone had paper and pencil out. Then she nodded at Mrs. O'Dowd and walked out the inside door.

I kept my eyes on my paper. A few tears dropped onto it and smeared the blue writing lines.

"Are you okay?" Paul whispered.

I shook my head, still staring at my paper. I couldn't look up. I wondered if anyone else was looking at me. I didn't feel like Louis anymore. I could hear them all saying, "Same old Billy Lou. Crying all over his desk." At least, I could hear them think it. I wiped my eyes with my sleeve.

Mrs. O'Dowd had a deep voice that went up and down, as if she were singing even when she was talking. I don't remember anything she said that morning. I just remember following that voice up and down. It was like climbing a lot of hills.

What happened to Mr. Forster? I kept hearing the

same question inside my head. I couldn't think of any answers that made sense. So the question kept asking itself, over and over again.

Until recess. Paul and I walked out to the playground with Veronica Allison and a large group of kids. Veronica had everyone's attention. "My mother says that Miss Cobb is being very tactful. She says it's the only way to handle the situation."

"I don't know what you're talking about," I said crossly.

Veronica looked pleased with herself. "Oh, don't you?" She gave Claudia a wink.

I felt like slapping her. "No, I don't."

"Billy Lou." Veronica said the name as if she were talking to a five-year-old. "Mr. Forster wasn't 'called away.' He was fired. And everybody knows why."

"I don't believe you. Why would Mr. Forster get fired? Just because people like Mrs. Siegel and Mrs. Hard..."—Claudia Hardcastle turned to give me a hateful look—"... some people don't like him. Mr. Forster's a good teacher. He's the best teacher in Kansas City."

Veronica rolled her eyes. "Mr. Forster's a queer."

Mickey Blake let out a laugh that sounded like a bark.

The knot in my stomach pulled tighter. I glanced at Paul. He had a sheepish grin on his face. I wanted to ask him what a queer was, but I couldn't. I could tell I was supposed to know already. I just said, "Mr. Forster isn't queer."

"Oh, yes, he is. He has a boyfriend and everything. They even live together. My mother said." Veronica curled a strand of her hair around one finger.

Suddenly Mickey Blake grabbed Robert Goldsmith and gave him a wet, noisy kiss on the face. Then he batted his eyelashes and started walking funny, with his hips swinging back and forth and one hand sticking out at his side. "Look at me, I'm Mr. Forster." Mickey made his voice kind of la-di-da and breathless. "Oh, Robert, will you be my boyfriend?"

Robert turned crimson. He gave a guilty-sounding laugh.

"You're crazy," I said. "Mr. Forster isn't like that at all." The knot in my stomach began to move.

Mickey stopped walking. "Hey." He sounded normal again. "Is Mr. Forster your boyfriend, Billy Lou? Maybe you're a queer, too. How about it, Lulubelle?"

Somebody gave a wolf whistle. I couldn't tell who.

"Looo—looo—belle." Mickey half shouted, half sang.

The knot in my stomach exploded.

I ran. Twice I hit my hand against the stone foundation of the school. I almost tripped on cracks in the asphalt. I saw the green outside doors leading to the bathroom. My hands pushed on them. I stumbled on the slippery floor.

I grabbed the sides of a toilet stall.

I threw up. I couldn't stop what was happening. I couldn't even stand up. The floor felt cold under my knees. I held down on the handle of the toilet, and the

153

constant flushing noise almost drowned out the sounds I was making.

I don't know how long it lasted. I just know that after a while, I noticed that it was quiet. My hand wasn't on the toilet anymore. I got up. I felt weak. As I washed my hands and face at the sink, I could smell those little white cubes the custodians put in all the toilets. The vomit smell was beginning to go away.

When I left the bathroom, I walked straight through the playground.

"Louis!" Paul waved to me from the sixth-grade play area.

I kept on going, down the short flight of steps at the back of the playground, onto the sidewalk, into the street. I couldn't stand to be at that school anymore. Not without Mr. Forster.

15

I didn't have a key, so I had to ring the doorbell when I got home. Aunt Zona answered it with a dust rag in one hand. "Why, Billy Lou! What are you doing home at this hour? You're not sick?"

I walked in and threw myself onto the sofa. The sunlight coming in through the living room windows made the cut glass candy dish on the coffee table twinkle. I lifted the lid and put it down again, twice, watching how flashes of light darted through it.

Aunt Zona lowered herself onto the edge of an easy chair. "What is it, punkin? Do you have a temperature? Why didn't you call me?"

"I'm not going back to that school. Ever."

Aunt Zona sat bolt upright. "Billy Lou Lamb, you're not telling me you're playing hookey from school. That's not like you."

"They fired Mr. Forster."

"Oh. So that's it." Aunt Zona sank back into the chair.

"You knew about it, didn't you." It wasn't a question. I just stared at Aunt Zona. For a minute, I think I hated her.

155

"Well, yes. I had a pretty good idea."

"Why, Aunt Zona?" I fought to keep the tears from coming back. "Mr. Forster's the best teacher I ever had. He didn't do anything wrong. Mr. Forster would never hurt anyone."

"Billy Lou. Mr. Foster is—he's just not fit to be around young people. When you're older, you'll understand better."

"Oh, no, I won't!" I shouted.

Aunt Zona's voice got cold. "Don't you use that tone with me, young man. I'll wash your mouth out with soap, see if I don't."

I jumped off the sofa. "It's not fair! It's not fair at all!"

Aunt Zona stood up, too. "People who are *that way* are an abomination in the sight of the Lord. You read your Bible. People like that Mr. Foster are headed straight to hell. First Corinthians 6:9."

"If Mr. Forster's going to hell, then I never want to go to heaven!"

"Billy Lou!" Aunt Zona looked as if she might hit me.

I ran to my room and slammed the door behind me. I waited to see if Aunt Zona would come after me. She didn't. The house was quiet. I wondered what Aunt Zona was doing now.

My china animals stood on the dresser. I took the unicorn in my hand. I held him up to the light. I wanted to crouch on the floor, spread the animals around me in a circle, make them dance. As if that would make everything all right.

But it wouldn't. Nothing could make everything all

right. My hand tightened around the unicorn's flanks. My hand was sweating, but I felt cold. I hadn't even taken my coat off, and I still felt cold.

I threw the unicorn down on the floor, hard. It broke into pieces. I took the lion and threw it down, too. Then the rhinoceros, and the tiger, and the giraffe. All the animals. I threw them all down as hard as I could. All of them cracked and broke. Heads and legs rolled under the dresser.

Aunt Zona called. She was coming down the hall. "Billy Lou, what are you doing in there? Billy Lou. Answer me!"

There was only one thing to do now. I had to find Mr. Forster. If I talked to him, maybe he could explain things to me. Maybe I could even make him come back to school. He could have it out with Miss Cobb and Mrs. Siegel and Mrs. Hardcastle. They'd have to see that they were wrong to fire him.

I threw my door open and ran right past Aunt Zona, into the dining room. I got the phone book and pulled out the little blue P.T.A. directory. I found Mr. Forster's address: 7324 Arcadia. I stuffed the directory into my coat pocket and headed for the front door.

Aunt Zona was still calling. Her voice sounded funny, as if she might be crying herself. "Billy Lou, you come right back here."

I ran out the door. I didn't stop running for three blocks, until I came to Prospect Avenue, where there was a bus stop. A Prospect Avenue bus was just coming up over the hill.

I got on. Luckily, I had dimes in my pocket. I dropped my money in the coin slot and found a seat.

It was a long ride up to Seventy-Third Street, then a seven or eight block walk west to Mr. Forster's house.

I felt strange. There were no kids in the yards of the houses I walked by, except for a few toddlers. Everyone was in school except me. It seemed like a police car ought to be following me, with Aunt Zona and Miss Cobb in the back seat, ready to jump out and drag me back to school. But the streets were practically empty.

7324 Arcadia turned out to be half of a duplex. I'd never pictured Mr. Forster living in a duplex. I walked up the sidewalk and rang the doorbell on Mr. Forster's side of the house.

I had to ring three times before the front door opened. A man stood there behind the glass storm door, the same man who had showed up in Room 3 on Open House night. Veronica had said Mr. Forster lived with his boyfriend. Which meant that this man was Mr. Forster's boyfriend. It was such a peculiar idea that I couldn't think of anything to say for a minute.

"Yes? What is it?" The man's voice sounded familiar. I'd heard it at school that time, of course. But now I realized that this was also the voice Paul and I had heard on the phone on Halloween when we called Mr. Forster. This was the man who had threatened to call the police. I almost turned right around and left. But I couldn't. I forced myself to talk.

"Is Mr. Forster here?" My voice sounded faint.

"I'm sorry. You can't see him. He's very busy."

158

"But I have to talk to him," I said. "Tell him Louis is here. I just want to see him. Just for a few minutes. Please."

"Who is it, Fred?" Mr. Forster came up behind the man in the doorway. "Louis. Why aren't you in school?"

"I couldn't stay there. Please, can I talk to you, Mr. Forster?"

"It's all right, Fred." Mr. Forster opened the storm door. "Come on in, Louis. If you've come all the way up here during school hours, it must be pretty important."

The other man stood to one side as I came in. He didn't look friendly at all. "I don't think this is such a good idea," he said to Mr. Forster. "Considering the circumstances."

Mr. Forster put a hand on the man's arm. "Don't worry. After all, things really can't get much worse than they already are, can they?" He closed both doors.

The man Fred didn't look convinced, but he left the room. "I'll be working upstairs," he called back.

"Let's go into the kitchen," Mr. Forster said. "We can talk there."

Mr. Forster's kitchen was full of plants. Plants on the floor, plants in window boxes, plants hanging from the ceiling. A small round table stood in front of one of the plant-filled windows. A half-filled cup of coffee and a package of Camel cigarettes sat on a slick yellow tablecloth. Next to the coffee was a big ceramic ashtray with three or four cigarette butts in it. This morning's *Kansas City Times* was folded up on one of the chairs.

159

"Sit down, Louis. I'll pour myself some more coffee. Would you like some milk or juice?"

I shook my head no and threw my coat over a chair. I sat.

While Mr. Forster was pouring the coffee, he asked, "Does your aunt know where you are?"

I shook my head again.

"I thought not. Before we do anything else, I'm going to call her."

I half stood up. "Oh, no. You can't."

"I have to. Use your head, Louis. You can't just run away from school and not tell anyone. Now what's your phone number?"

I told him. There was a phone on a table just outside the kitchen door. Mr. Forster called Aunt Zona. They talked for a few minutes. When he hung up, Mr. Forster brought his coffee to the kitchen table and sat down. "Your Aunt Zona is very worried about you," Mr. Forster said. "She'll be here to pick you up in a little while. Meanwhile, we can have our talk. I guess I don't have to ask what's on your mind." Mr. Forster took a long sip of coffee. He seemed very calm, although his mouth was set in kind of a line, and his eyes looked tired.

For a minute I wondered what Aunt Zona would do when she got here. Then I decided I didn't have time to worry about that. "Mr. Forster, Veronica Allison says that you got fired."

Mr. Forster took another sip of coffee. He lit a cigarette. "That's right, Louis."

I didn't see how he could be so matter-of-fact about

160

it. "But you're a good teacher!" I said. "How can they do that to you?"

Mr. Forster blew out some smoke. "Did Veronica mention why I was fired?"

I blushed. I couldn't help it. "She said you were a queer."

Mr. Forster gave a sour little grin. "I don't like that word, Louis. It's an ugly word, like *nigger*. But Veronica's right about that, too."

I swallowed, hard. "But—" There didn't seem to be anything I could say.

"Louis, I'm a homosexual. Do you understand what that means?"

I shook my head.

"It's not an easy thing to explain," Mr. Forster said. "Especially to someone your age. I'm not exactly sure that I even want to try. For now, just try to understand that there are many ways of loving. You met my friend at the door. Fred and I love each other. That's the important thing for you to understand now. When you get older—"

"That's what Aunt Zona said," I interrupted. "*When I'm older*. Aunt Zona said that—she said that people like you are going to—well, not going to heaven."

Mr. Forster let out a short, tight laugh. "I wouldn't know about that," he said. "I think I'll wait and let God come to his own decision about my eternal destiny. But I might add that I don't think I'm any more sinful than most ordinary folk."

I poked my finger at a coffee stain on the yellow tablecloth. "I just don't think they should fire you. I think you should come back to school and fight for your rights. You belong there."

Mr. Forster sighed. "I'm afraid you're wrong about that, Louis. I'm beginning to realize that I never fit in very well at Alcott School, and not just because I'm homosexual. I didn't see eye to eye with a lot of the adults I worked with. I'm sorry to say that the world looks very different to them than it does to me."

"But how can you just quit teaching?"

"Oh, Louis. Sometimes we have to do things we don't want to do. Of course I don't want to quit teaching. I like teaching. I like kids. I always have. But in this situation, I have no choice. The decision has been made for me. After this, it would be almost impossible for me to get another teaching job anywhere else."

I was not going to cry in Mr. Forster's kitchen. I simply was not. "What will you do now?" I asked, rubbing the coffee stain.

"That," said Mr. Forster, drawing on his cigarette, "is the Sixty-four Thousand Dollar Question. I might go back to Virginia. Or I might try to get some other kind of job here."

"But what about me?" My voice almost broke in spite of everything. "What am I going to do now? When you were my teacher . . ." *Were.* It hurt to say *were.* ". . . things were different. The other kids started treating me differently. They called me Louis."

"That's because they began to recognize you for who you are," Mr. Forster said gently. "You don't need me to learn how to be yourself. You're finding that out on your own, every day."

162

"You don't know what it's like. Now that you're gone, they've started calling me Billy Lou again. Mickey Blake even called me 'Lulubelle.' That's worse than Billy Lou. Now the whole year was all for nothing. It was all just a big waste."

Mr. Forster didn't say anything for a moment or two. He drank some more coffee. Then he turned his chair so that he was looking directly into my eyes. "It doesn't have to be a waste," Mr. Forster said. "Nothing is a waste, not if you know how to make it mean something."

I looked down, but Mr. Forster went right on talking.

"Listen to me, Louis. There's a way for you to make sense out of all this, out of everything that's happened. But you have to find it for yourself. And when you find it, it's like—well, it's like what Reverend Hardcastle might call *grace*. It doesn't make all the bad things go away. But it makes you know that everything matters. That it's all worth something. That nothing is ever really lost."

The doorbell rang. I let out a shaky breath. "I guess that's Aunt Zona," I said.

"I guess so." Mr. Forster smiled at me. He reached out and ruffled my hair. Then he got up to answer the door.

I just sat there for a minute. I tried to figure out what Mr. Forster had been saying. Mr. Forster said that I could make sense out of everything that had happened. But I couldn't. Nothing made sense. It never would. Nothing meant anything at all.

163

16

I could tell that Aunt Zona was really upset. She'd come to Mr. Forster's in a taxicab. Aunt Zona never took taxicabs. She said the fares were highway robbery. But she let this one stand with the meter running while she collected me from Mr. Forster's kitchen.

Mr. Forster and Aunt Zona didn't say much to each other. They both looked a little uncomfortable. But as we were going down the walk, Mr. Forster called, "That's a fine boy you have there, Mrs. Crenshaw. One of these days he'll make you very proud of him."

Aunt Zona looked back. She nodded slowly. Then we got into the cab. As we pulled away, Mr. Forster waved.

On the way home, Aunt Zona didn't do any of the things I thought she'd do. She didn't yell at me. She didn't talk about punishing me. She just put her arm around me and listened while I talked about Mr. Forster.

As the cab pulled up in front of our house, Aunt Zona said, "I think your Mr. Foster is really good at heart. Maybe the Lord will forgive him for being *that way*."

For the rest of that day, I was so sleepy I could

164

hardly stay awake. Aunt Zona let me go to my room and read. My bedroom floor was clean. No trace of my china animals. I didn't ask Aunt Zona what she had done with the pieces. I didn't want to know.

That night I went to bed early, right after supper. Aunt Zona came in and felt my forehead. "No temperature," she said. "But maybe you ought to stay home from school tomorrow, punkin, just in case."

I was so surprised, I felt wide awake for a minute. Aunt Zona didn't sound like Aunt Zona at all. She stroked my hair. Usually I wouldn't let her do that. But tonight I didn't feel like pushing her hand away. I just let her keep on stroking, until finally I fell asleep.

The next day, Aunt Zona didn't wake me at the usual time. When I opened my eyes, I could tell it was late. I could hear rustling noises out in the kitchen, but no singing. There had never been a morning when Aunt Zona didn't sing. Not until now.

At breakfast, Aunt Zona was quiet and serious. She seemed to be watching me, but at the same time she left me alone, in a way she never had before. I wasn't sure I liked it.

Aunt Zona didn't say anything about getting dressed. I waited until after ten o'clock. Then I got out an old shirt and a pair of blue jeans. In one of my dresser drawers, I saw the notebook with the black-and-white cover. The one Mr. Forster had given me when I wrote the story about the marvelous Mr. Mystifaction.

After I got dressed, I took the notebook out. I flipped

through the pages. They were still blank. I had never been able to think of anything to write on them. I rubbed my hand against the rough black tape that covered the binding stitches.

I still wasn't sure what to do with the notebook, but I decided to keep it with me all day. I sat on my bed, with the notebook at my side, and finished reading both of the Hardy Boys books Aunt Zona had given me for Christmas. Sometimes I looked up to rest my eyes. I thought about the things Mr. Forster had said in his kitchen. They still didn't make much sense.

The day went by faster than I expected. At 4:00, Paul called me. He wanted to know if I was sick. I said I guessed not. I told him I would probably be back at school tomorrow. When I said that, I realized that it was true. I was actually going to do it. I was going to walk back into Room 3, and I'd be in Mrs. O'Dowd's class, not Mr. Forster's. It was really going to happen that way, no matter how strange and impossible it seemed.

The next morning, things were almost normal again.

Aunt Zona got me up at the regular time. She sang, too. Not "Billy Boy," though. Something about "amazing grace."

When I left for school, I took the black-and-white notebook along. Somehow it made me feel better to have it in my hand. It was like carrying a weapon into Room 3 with me.

It was too cold a morning for kids to stand outside

166

and wait for the bell to ring. When I got to school, everybody was already in the room, taking off hats and coats, or just sitting around, talking, while Mrs. O'Dowd copied some arithmetic problems onto a square of blackboard.

Paul was at his desk, sketching something on the back of a tablet. He smiled when I sat down. "I'm inventing a new superhero," he said. "When I figure out who he is, maybe you and I can do a book about him."

I shrugged. "Maybe," I said. I put the notebook in my desk.

Nobody asked me where I'd been. Nobody talked about Mr. Forster, either. They were all talking about Mrs. O'Dowd, how easy she was, and how much fun it was to fool her.

"I wrote my whole English homework assignment in invisible ink," Robert Goldsmith was saying. "Just wait till she sees it. I'm going to give her the paper and a book of matches, so she can read it."

Mickey Blake snickered. "Hi, Lulubelle," he said over his shoulder.

Veronica Allison glanced at me and laughed.

Paul looked up sharply. "Leave him alone, Blake. Or else you can step outside and watch me beat your brains in."

Mickey went back to talking with Robert and Veronica and a couple of other kids. He didn't say anything more to me.

Paul touched my arm. "You shouldn't pay any atten-

167

tion to people like Mickey Blake and Veronica Allison," he said. "They're probably just jealous, anyway."

I grunted. I knew Mickey Blake and Veronica Allison had no reason at all to be jealous of me. "What gets me," I said after a while, "is how they can just sit there as if nothing had happened. Doesn't anybody care about Mr. Forster?"

"Well, God, Louis." Paul sighed. "Okay, Mr. Forster is a nice man. He's even a pretty good teacher, as teachers go. But after all, he *is* a queer." Paul gave me the kind of look you give someone like Ellie Siegel, someone who isn't quite all there. It wasn't a mean look. In fact, it was sort of a sad look. As if I didn't really know what I was saying.

That reminded me. I looked over at Ellie's desk. She was back. Now that I thought about it, I remembered seeing her on Monday, too. Nobody was talking to Ellie, of course. She had her head behind a book about Cherry Ames, student nurse. It occurred to me that if it hadn't been for Ellie and her mother, Mr. Forster might never have been fired. Yet somehow that didn't make me mad at Ellie.

"Oh, Louis," Mrs. O'Dowd said in her deep voice. "By my records, it's your turn to put up the Thought for the Day. Would you write it on the board before the tardy bell rings, please?"

I stood up. I got *Bartlett's Familiar Quotations* from Mr. Forster's—no, Mrs. O'Dowd's—desk and thumbed through it until I found something I liked. Then I walked to the blackboard and wrote it out.

Thought for the Day
The world is a comedy to those that think,
a tragedy to those who feel.
Horace Walpole.

The tardy bell rang.

I stood at the blackboard and watched as everyone started to copy my Thought. Veronica Allison. Robert Goldsmith. Claudia Hardcastle. Mickey Blake. Ellie Siegel. Paul.

Nothing is a waste, Mr. Forster had said. Not if you know how to make it mean something. Nothing is ever really lost.

I walked slowly back to my desk. Everyone around me was writing. The points of their cartridge pens scratched against clean notebook paper.

And that's when it came to me.

I knew. What do do. How to make everything mean something, so that, as Mr. Forster said, nothing would be really lost.

I reached inside my desk and took out the notebook Mr. Forster had given me. I touched the cover that looked like black marble. I opened the notebook to the first page and ran my hand over the slick blank paper. Then I took out my pen, but not to write down the Thought for the Day.

I wrote about Mr. Forster.

ABOUT THE AUTHOR

Gary W. Bargar was born and raised in Kansas City, Missouri. He has been an elementary school teacher and an editor at several large educational publishing houses. Currently, Mr. Bargar lives in New York City, where he works as a free-lance writer and editor. *What Happened to Mr. Forster?* is his first novel.